# Some Silent Hero

Part I of a trilogy

Stephanie Brookes

SPIRITUAL PHILOSOPHY PUBLISHING LIMITED

Published by:
SPIRITUAL PHILOSOPHY PUBLISHING LIMITED
PO Box 79
Midhurst
West Sussex
GU29 9WW

Spiritual Philosophy Publishing website:
www.spiritualphilosophy.co.uk

A catalogue record for this book is available from the British Library

ISBN 0-9548959-0-8

All papers used by the publisher are natural, recyclable products derived
from wood grown in sustainable forests.

Typesetting and design by Cecil Smith, RPM, Chichester.
Set in Baskerville.

Printed and bound in Great Britain by Cambridge University Press.

The publisher wishes to thank every individual and company that has
helped put this book into print. Thank you all so much.

## Acknowledgements

For the people who have helped me along the way
I would like to thank:

Dad, for suggesting that we start a company and
publish the book ourselves.

Mum, for reading my early stories and encouraging
me through my most exciting project.

Rick, my number one bruv! Your financial
assistance has been greatly appreciated by your
poverty-stricken sis'.

James, thank you for your love and inspiration
throughout the two years of writing this book.

Leone and Alan, for telling me to keep writing.

Cecil, for his unfailing patience and guidance.

My wonderful friends and family.

Dedication – to my Spiritual Mentor

To the memory of an inspirational and passionate soul
for whom all things seemed possible.
The great Vivien Leigh.

# Prologue

DAD ONCE told me that we are all watched over by silent heroes. I imagined a tall, cowboy-like figure in the mould of John Wayne striding alongside me on my way home from school. That, I discovered much later in life, wasn't the case. It was more likely that a relative who had passed into Spirit was looking over my shoulder; but I hadn't ruled out John Wayne altogether. Mum always scowled when Dad and I talked about the possibility of Spirits watching over us. She wanted nothing to do with these 'silly stories' and believed my Dad should concentrate on more important things like supporting the family, which he did.

For money, my Dad worked most of his life for a coffee company. Ironic really, as coffee was his least favourite drink. It was, however, one of my Mum's staple food sources, in fact, it was her saviour. Coffee was my family's means of survival. The aroma filled the house daily. As young as I was, the deep woody smells of freshly perked coffee thrilled my senses.

I was just eight years old when my world changed. It happened one sweltering night in June. I remember the night clearly as we had just returned from Rena's birthday party. I was sitting up in bed, with the light dimmed, counting the sweets in my party bag, quite oblivious to the noisy conversation that was taking place downstairs. My Mum had a loud voice in any case and I had learnt to ignore it.

"I hate you Simon! Why don't you just leave?"

I bit hard on my tongue instead of my toffee. I wondered what they could be shouting about now? Mum and Dad often had these play fights and tonight I was curious to find out more. I jumped out of my bed, took a front row seat at the top of the stairs, and peered down at my parents below. I thought I'd wait five more minutes before I would join in the fun. It was still early after all; we'd only just got back from the party.

"For heaven's sake, lower your voice," Dad growled.

"I'll raise my voice whenever I want to."

"It's no longer about you and me Joanna. We have an eight year old daughter to think about too."

It was very funny listening to them but they sounded ever so serious. Dad always said that Mum had a flair for the dramatics and I was creased up with laughter. I was ready to explode.

"This really is the last straw Simon and don't use my daughter as an excuse. I'm sick of you dodging the issue!"

"And what might that be?"

"That you don't love me any more. I just don't love you any more."

I didn't feel like laughing any more. Mum's final words were my cue to return quietly to my bedroom, where I should have been all along. I wish I hadn't listened in. I didn't understand their words but I understood the horrible atmosphere. I was eight years old and powerless to do anything. I reached into my toy box, gathered all my favourite soft animals and placed them around my pillow. I hugged teddy close and talked to him; we drifted off to sleep together.

I believe a fresh new morning can counterbalance a previous bad night. As I woke, the sun burst through the curtains and the cross words exchanged by my parents were momentarily forgotten. I felt a sudden burst of unimaginable happiness like one experiences on Christmas morning; magical moments before the initial present is hastily unwrapped. I looked into my pink-rimmed mirror and flattened my hair, making my round face look even rounder, and headed for the door.

Creeping silently downstairs was a trick I used when my parents had been arguing. They loved me to surprise them, as it made them laugh and made me feel like I was being particularly clever. On this occasion there was no forum for my friendly attack. I stood at the foot of the stairs stock-still. The blood in my veins froze, and all I could do was stand and stare. The door, which led out onto the patio, was open. A sharp breeze whipped through the hall cutting at my face with the smell of alcohol and discarded cigarettes. All I wanted to do was to step over my Mum sprawled across the rug and dart straight to my swing. She was in the same peach coloured dress that she had worn at the party the night before. A lonely bottle lay in its own pale yellow liquid. The thing that bothered me most was her hair; it looked like a heap of rats' tails, her blonde highlights looked dirty.

For a moment I felt angry. She always moaned that my hair was knotty, and should be combed more often. But to look at her now made me feel sick and confused. What was she doing down there? Why now, when my Dad wasn't around to pick her up and put her to bed. I was alone with my drunken Mum. I moved closer to her and kneeled beside her. She smelt greasy and as I touched her arm she murmured. I sat there, stroking her hair, waiting for my Dad's return.

And so it continued, a new pattern had emerged from that Saturday morning. A routine of shouting matches and smashed bottles. I never could understand why she chose to drink so much; all I knew was that coffee, temporarily, helped her. It would 'sober' her up. I didn't know what the word meant at the time, however, my Dad would say this word when speaking about my Mum's recovery. I knew that coffee plus 'sober' equalled a Mum who would be awake enough to watch cartoons with me.

My ninth birthday couldn't have come quicker. It wasn't the cake or the presents I was eager for, it was the fact that I would be growing older and hopefully taller. I would be able to do more for my Mum, even collect the weekly essentials from our local convenience store. It was about this time that the roles in our home began to shift. I had made a decision to do all that I could to help my parents. Dad was at a loss with what to do with my Mum. I knew this, from a conversation overheard between him and my Grandma Joyce. It was a difficult conversation to understand. I had to hold my breath so as not to be heard.

"I know what we agreed but it's getting worse every day. Vivien sees it all, I don't know what must be going through her head. I realise what I promised but I don't know how many more years I can stand it." Dad looked dejected. Grandma wiped her tears. I knew then what I had to do; I had to make my bed every day, not nag my Mum to watch cartoons with me and not whine when I was told to go to bed. I had to remain as silent as the grave. In order to keep my parents together I had to remain as silent and strong as John Wayne. I had to be a hero.

## Twelve Years Later...

THE TAXI driver shuffled uncomfortably in his seat. He had only been on his shift for twenty minutes but already his thick, sweat-laden jeans were beginning to chafe at his crotch. Hoards of rowdy teenage girls passed his window. He watched as they hobbled by on strappy stilettos. One particular blonde caught his eye. He watched her buns pressed tightly against her white PVC skirt until the girlish laughs and shouts faded as they turned a corner. He resigned himself to the fact that five hours would pass until those girls would, once again, pass the taxi rank. Next time they would open the door and pour into the back seat of his cab. It was sad, but they were never as attractive when they had downed twelve shots and polished off a crate of alchopops. Billy was in for another long, long shift.

He slouched further down his seat, his knees pressing

forcibly against the steering wheel. It was an uncomfortable position to relax into, but after seven years of mastering the art of uncomfortable sleep he was used to it.

As he began to shut off from the rowdy Saturday night crowd, a muffled but very deliberate banging on his window disturbed him. He turned and saw a sight he hadn't expected until at least 11.15pm. He wound down his window and was greeted with the strong smell of hard alcohol.

"Where are you going to, love?"

The young woman leaned in the direction of Billy's haggard face. Through her blurred vision she resigned herself to the fact that, 'He would do'.

"You've definitely 'ad too many. You stand up properly or you're gonna fall and hurt yourself."

He watched as the girl staggered round the front of the taxi, keeping her left hand firmly on the bonnet for balance. As she slid round he could tell it was going to be a feat to even open the door. In fact, it took three attempts. On the fourth she launched herself onto the back seat and tugged the door shut with a well-trained foot.

"You can't stay like that. I'm not going anywhere unless you sit up proper."

"Shit."

"What did you say miss?"

"I said I'd shit up properly."

Her unfortunate slip of the tongue brought a smile to his face. He wafted a chubby hand in front of her face in an attempt to alert her to the fact that a seat belt would be another condition to them actually moving out of the taxi rank.

"I'm belted up now. Any chance of movement?" she said with a smile.

"Where am I taking you to?"

"Home James, because I'm drunk, ha ha!"

"Very funny, where's home?"

"My home is near an airport – next to an airport – just think airport."

"I'll drive you as far as Winter Road which is next to the airport but you'd better think fast because I'll be there in ten minutes."

He should have refused point blank to drive her anywhere without an address but he could tell she was not more than twenty years old and definitely not equipped to spend the night on a park bench. At least she was a happy drunk.

"So, had a good night? It's a little early to be going home?"

He looked through his mirror, half expecting a response but was not in the least surprised that her eyes were rolling back and forth – inebriated to the hilt.

"Out with friends?"

"Not that I can remember."

"What was that love? Say again."

"I was on my own. Enjoying a private conversation."

"You ought to be out with friends."

"Brad stood me up. Keanu missed his flight. So I drank for them as well."

She might have been drunk but at least she was coherent. Billy glanced in the mirror again, in part, to check her face. As he looked closer he saw a very attractive woman sitting on his back seat. A swarm of long dark locks hung off her shoulders; had they seen a good brush she would have looked even better. Her features were of perfect proportion, especially her cupid's bow lips. Had she been a little older he might have turned on the charm.

"I think I'm going to lie down for a bit."

"Not going to be sick?" Billy hoped.

He watched as she curled up. Any sign of retching and he was ready to blast his horn. He felt slightly relieved that she had fallen asleep. For the time being he could cruise the dual carriageway in total silence. A quiet stretch of road was what he loved best, he had to restrain himself from pressing the accelerator any further, he was still on duty after all.

"Now, where's that big old rich street Winter Road?" he mumbled, not entirely sure if he was turning into the right road. The streets were dimly lit and the curtains tightly shut. Security cameras adorned the tree-lined street.

"Rich bastards!" Billy grumbled, as he turned into Winter Road. "Wake up now. This is the longest road in the area. You need to tell me if you live near here?"

Billy pulled up by a curb under the glare of a lonesome street light. He wound down his window to let in the fresh evening air.

"It's very near here."

"Look love, you need to tell me where you live. How about this street, look familiar?"

Billy slouched in his seat and wiped his forehead with a crumpled handkerchief. This could turn out to be a very long night.

"Mr Taxi man, I'm going to show you something."

She tipped the contents of her bag onto the back seat, rummaged through until she found a small cream card, and handed it over to Billy.

"This yer business card?" he asked with mild curiosity. "Oh, I see, this is where you live, 10 Willow Court, Ossilton. Well, that's easy enough, just off Winter Road then."

Billy handed the card back. As soon as she had taken it, she curled up yet again.

"Do you have a name by the way?"

"Vivien. But people call me Viv."

"My mother's name; I love that name." Billy warmed to his passenger.

Just off Winter Road was the more subdued Willow Court, a tiny cul-de-sac made up of red brick houses which all looked just the same.

"I call this Clone Court. Boring isn't it?"

"I think it's very nice."

Billy pulled up outside number ten. The only thing that separated this house from the rest was the unkempt and withered look about the place. Unlike the other houses it had no decorative features, no flowers and an untidy garden. The only sign of life was a bright light that had been deliberately left on for Viv's return.

"Ten fifty love. Don't bother with the fifty though."

"Thanks," she mumbled as she opened every zip on her bag to find that elusive tenner. She found it eventually in the first pocket she had opened, mixed up with a piece of old tissue.

"Thanks for getting me home..."

"Billy's my name."

"Thank you, Billy."

"Need a hand to the door?"

"I'll be alright," she fibbed, gripped the door handle, stumbled slightly and then slammed it shut. "It's funny isn't it?"

"What is?"

"I was really drunk an hour ago and it's nearly worn off. I feel much better now."

She still stumbled towards the front door and just hoped her mother wouldn't be waiting on the other side. Billy drove away hoping the rest of the night's passengers would be as pleasant as Viv.

◆

VIV HAD lived in the same house since she was born. The material aspect hadn't altered much. She was still wiping her shoes on the same mat she had wiped her shoes on for the last twenty-one years. She felt sentimental towards what the house represented. It was part of her life; there was no escaping it.

Tonight, she wanted nothing more than to reflect on what had happened that evening. With every sip of alcohol she realised she was becoming more and more like her mother. The thought sent a chill down her spine as she put the key in the door. Luckily, the coast was clear. Viv kicked off her painful stilettos. One size too small but half price in the sale, her feet looked like a sliced loaf. She hobbled towards the kitchen in the direction of the kettle, flicked the switch and waited for the low rumble to start. A cup containing one heaped teaspoon of coffee had already been put on the worktop. Her mother performed the same ritual every time Viv went to the pub. Coffee in hand, she carefully made her way over to the sofa.

"I can't believe it's only nine! How long have I been drinking then?" she wondered. It was confusing, had she really been drinking since happy hour? Arriving home at this hour was embarrassing. Her embarrassment grew as she reflected on the conversations with her late afternoon drinking companions. Alfred's war stories were the best, but then again he had drunk three pints of Guinness more than anybody else had downed. At 5pm he was a captain of the artillery in the Welsh Fusiliers and by 6pm he was a tank commander and a desert rat. Charles was not quite as drunk and noted that, "Alfred wasn't a desert rat. He was just pissed as a rat." Percy who was the most sober, drinking a concoction of port wine and raw eggs, revealed in a whisper that they'd actually all been delivery men in the Co-op, and had to ask for help loading their rifles on the Shooting Gallery on Brighton Pier. Viv loved their stories. A Saturday afternoon wasn't quite the same without their company.

As she sat up, her knees knocked the edge of the table, tipping the coffee over, drowning the newspapers and magazines in one clumsy motion. "Great," she sighed, trying frantically to mop the spill with an out of date newspaper, before it spattered the carpet. Throwing the magazines aside she spotted a newspaper cutting she hadn't seen in months. She turned it over to reveal a piece of smudged writing. Her heart skipped a beat, she picked up the article, still covered in finger marks, her finger marks.

*'Last known photograph taken of*
*Simon Goddard. Santa Monica Beach,*
*California. January 10th 2002.'*

As Viv read, the memory of the ordeal manifested in the pit of her stomach, she retreated to the sofa and curled up in the corner.

"Baby is that you?"

"Of course it's me," she sighed wearily.

"Vivien?"

"I'm here Mum, in the lounge."

"I thought I heard a noise," she said cheerily. "Why are you back so early? I thought you and Rena would be painting the town red."

"She's at her Dad's this weekend. I went drinking with my other mates."

"Who are they then?" Joanna enquired.

"Never mind." Viv cringed.

Viv sensed her mother hovering, so she turned to face her. She was sad that her mother never bothered to tend to her appearance any more. Her peroxide hair looked old and dingy. In fact, it hadn't changed at all, for as long as Viv could remember. She hadn't removed her make-up either, her eyes smudged with black mascara. Her mother seemed fragile now. Her once expressive voice had been replaced with uncertainty. Now she seemed like a china doll perched upon the top shelf, ready for the push and there was nothing Viv could do to prevent it. Since her father's sudden death, she had watched her mother succumb to alcoholism. It had become progressively worse with each passing day. The agony of watching her deteriorate was too much. Viv knew that the only way to help her mother was to encourage her every day. She had learnt that telling her not to drink, only made matters worse.

"How was your evening Mum?"

"Fine. I missed you."

"Did you do anything interesting?"

"I had an idea earlier. How about tomorrow we sort out your A level certificates? We could get them framed on Monday. Something we could do together."

Viv wriggled further down the sofa, the question had put her on tenterhooks.

"In fact, sweetie, I don't think I've seen your certificates since you passed your exams."

"I did show them to you Mum. Maybe you forgot," Viv lied and hoped that her mothers's long-term memory failed to register that fact. "Can we talk about it tomorrow? I'm feeling tired."

"I know sweetie, sleep well."

Once her mother was out of sight she retrieved the

newspaper cutting from under the cushion and looked at it once again; lingering on her father's beaming smile. She even mustered a chuckle. He looked so silly in the picture, sporting a baseball cap with huge horns coming from either side. He had gone on a business trip to the United States with his colleagues. They were always joking around and fooling about. On this particular day he had telephoned Viv. The conversation was still crystal clear in her memory.

*"The weather out here is fantastic sweetpea. You and Rena should come out for a holiday."*

*"We will Dad."*

*"Is your Mum okay, any problems?"*

*"She's a raving loony but I can handle her,"* she smiled, *"So, what are you up to today?"*

*"Well, as it's Saturday, Ron, Mike and myself are headed for the beach. We're going to pick up some babes."*

*"Hey!"*

*"I'm only kidding."*

*"Have you been to Disneyland, yet?"*

*"We haven't gone as far as Anaheim. Maybe next weekend."*

*"I envy you Dad. I wish I were there. Oh, make sure you use your sun block, remember the lobster incident in Portugal?"*

*"I remember, I couldn't sit down for a month."*

*"That was so funny."*

*"Viv, I'll have to go as my credit's running out. Speak to you soon, sweetheart. Remember to keep revising. No partying."*

*"I love you, lobster."*

*"I love you too, smart ass."*

The conversation was brief but it had stayed with Viv. He sounded happy. The simple knowledge that he was headed to the beach and not some meeting was a blessing and she was grateful. His ambitions were never materialistic, only to fill as many happy times into his life as possible.

Viv was feeling almost sober now. The night's events were beginning to come into focus. She felt sad. Her hands were marked with sticky black mascara and her thoughts were, once again, with her father. His passing had caused a gaping hole in her existence. She was determined not to be defeated though. She was going to be strong not only for herself but for her mother too.

◆

RENA PADULA was Viv's best friend. They had known each other since they were four years of age when Rena and her mother, Carmen, had moved into the house next door. They were like a breath of fresh air when they moved into Willow Court, they always said 'good morning' and never had a bad word to say about anybody, unlike many of the old crones that made up the rest of the cul-de-sac.

"Good morning Viv. How has your weekend been so far?" Carmen called out. She took off her gardening gloves and walked over to her neighbour.

"Alright thanks. Is Rena around?"

"She's still at her father's. She'll be back first thing Monday morning."

Viv managed a smile. She felt uncomfortable that she was still wearing the black mini-skirt from the night before.

"How is your mother?"

"Mum's fine, thanks."

"And you?"

"Had an interesting night out, it's a shame Rena wasn't there."

"You must be chilly in that little outfit." Carmen smiled knowingly.

"I am a bit, I better get going then, my white legs are enough to put anyone off their breakfast."

As Viv turned around she noticed the blatant stares from behind the hedges of house number fourteen and shot the Suttons a glance before heading for the shops.

Her mother was already in the kitchen when she returned.

"No tea for me then Mum?"

"I thought you only drank coffee Vivien?"

"Well, I wouldn't say no to a tea."

"You drank too much last night, didn't you?"

"I didn't do anything wrong."

"I wish you didn't drink so much," she said breathlessly. Although Joanna thought she'd had this conversation many times with Viv; if the truth were known, Viv rarely got drunk at all.

"I don't see how there's a problem with it. I go out and

occasionally have one too many. Most people of my age are doing it every weekend."

Joanna felt a little guilty.

"In truth Mum, the person with the problem is you. I don't want to seem rude," she added, "but it has to be addressed."

"How about we sort out your certificates today. Remember, I mentioned it to you last night?"

"Mum, don't change the subject."

"Tea, darling?"

Viv no longer wanted the tea. She needed a breather from her mother and her constant refusal to acknowledge her problem. After a quick change of clothes she headed towards her old Peugeot. Her father had given it to her before he departed for America. Initially its shoddy paint-work and torn upholstered seats disappointed her, but since his death she had cherished the little car as if it were her own baby. As she turned on the ignition she realised it hadn't seen a soapy sponge for a while, and made a mental note to clean it when she could face returning home.

Café Latte, Cappuccino and Mocha? What happened to a cup of coffee, she wondered.

"Can I help you?"

"Coffee, with milk please."

"Large?" he said looking over his shoulder to the clock behind him.

"Yes."

"Two twenty."

As she rifled through her coat pocket it was apparent that the twenty was going to be hard to come by.

"Do you accept cards?"

"No we don't."

"Just one moment, I must have a twenty somewhere."

As she fumbled she heard the exasperated sighs of the queue behind her.

"I'm very sorry about this, I have two pounds but I can't find the twenty."

Just as she was beginning to give up hope, a twenty pence piece was slid onto the marble counter. She turned around.

"Thank you very much. How nice of you."

"You're welcome," a man replied.

Viv meekly took her coffee over to a small table ideally placed to inspect the person who had shown her generosity. A man in his late twenties, with black shiny hair was certainly easy on the eyes. He was really handsome but not in a 'look at me' conventional way. A really handsome man would have said, 'Hurry up!' and would never have dreamt of helping out anyone but himself. As she took her first sip, she felt her cheeks flush. The kind stranger sat down only a few tables away from her. As she leaned over to the next table to grab a newspaper his mobile phone rang.

"It's perfectly safe man. Don't worry so much, she's sat outside and loving all the attention."

Viv's curiosity was tweaked. She craned her neck to see who was the mysterious 'she'. It turned out to be a motorbike.

"Anyway man, my drink's getting cold. I'll bring her round later."

Viv turned back to her newspaper, but caught his eye.

"Thank you for the twenty pence by the way."

"It's my pleasure," he smiled kindly.

"I would pay you back but…"

"It's my pleasure," he laughed and looked down towards his newspaper.

Maybe she shouldn't have said anything in the first place. 'God, I say some stupid stuff!' she thought and pretended to read the newspaper. As she sipped the coffee she felt that she was being watched. It made her drink up and turn the pages quickly. Not that she minded being watched by a handsome man, but it felt oddly like staring. Her eyes fell upon an article on page eighteen, the picture of her father was unmistakable. An article written by his former colleagues, paid tribute to *a dear friend and associate, who will never be forgotten and is sorely missed'*. The article coincided with her father's birthday, something she had tried not to focus on.

"Interesting article?"

Viv looked up.

"Sure. Fantastic."

"You look consumed. I was just wondering what page you're reading. I take it you're not reading about the Ossilton Fishing Championship!"

Viv couldn't help smiling, but she refrained from giving the page number, as it would invite too many questions.

"Thanks for helping me out earlier, but I better get

going. Good luck with the fishing article."

As Viv left the shop, the anonymous Good Samaritan pulled the discarded paper into view glancing at the articles on page eighteen. Something clicked immediately, the name Simon Goddard was very familiar. He tore the article from the newspaper and dashed out of the coffee shop, nearly knocking the bike down as he sped out. He looked around but the street was empty. She had vanished.

◆

"TO BE perfectly honest Dad, I don't believe in this stuff. Why did you want me to come?" Rena asked.

"Because Rena, I want you to be an open-minded young woman and be able to think for yourself. Only when a person has knowledge can they decide what they believe in and what they don't."

"Dad, I'm twenty-one years old."

"I know that and you'd rather be down the pub with Vivien."

Rena didn't like to admit it, but that was exactly what she had been thinking. Maybe her father was psychic or spiritual or whatever the thing was.

"How long until the service starts?" she asked.

"The service starts in five minutes."

Rena had enjoyed the weekend so far, but now she was sat in a Spiritualist Church waiting impatiently for something to happen.

"Will we all sit around a table and link hands and wait

for it to start moving?" she joked.

"That could well be one reason why I brought you here today. So many people have preconceived ideas about matters they have no knowledge of."

"Lighten up Dad." Rena felt frustrated.

Sajeet turned to his daughter and smiled. He was a little uptight; he knew it, probably a little set in his ways. He checked the time once again and waited patiently for the service to begin.

Rena's thoughts were with Viv a moment later, however, it felt good to be on her own for one weekend. It was starting to feel like they were attached at the hip, they were drinking partners, dinner partners, gossip partners, the list went on and on.

"So what is going to happen tonight?"

"You're just about to find out."

That night Viv had a very unappetising meal of cold beans on stale toast. There wasn't anything else in the house, and though she really fancied something nice to eat she wasn't in the mood for a take-away.

"What have you been up to today?" Joanna yawned at the bottom of the stairs.

"Nothing much," she replied as bean juice dribbled down her chin. She caught her mother's eye and was taken aback. Joanna glared at Viv.

"Do you know what I've been up to today?"

Viv glared back, she had never seen her mother so distraught. The alcohol usually made her so relaxed in comparison.

"What's happened?"

"Despite what you told me about your results, I decided to see for myself. Just to bask in my daughter's recent success, and to my astonishment I found..." she faltered and bit her lip. "That you failed! You failed every one of your exams!"

"Mum calm down, let me explain."

"Explain what? You lied to me. You failed your finals again and you have no hope of getting into a university let alone a decent one! You've been messing around for years. You're almost twenty-two!"

Viv put her fork down and forced herself to listen.

"How could you, Vivien? So all this talk about a gap year before deciding on a university is all part of some plan to fool your silly mother. I bet you had it all figured out. You could work all year and then decide conveniently that you don't want to go after all. Is that it?" she screamed and staggered over to the fridge where she took out a bottle of opened wine.

"Mum don't start, please. I can explain. I didn't want to tell you because I knew you'd be disappointed. I'm going to see about re-sitting them. Why do you think I'm at college all the time? I want to pass."

"I'm sure. Tomorrow you'll be saying something completely different. I can tell how this is going to turn out. Oh, I can tell," she stuttered in anger.

"I can't talk to you about this. I can't talk to you about anything can I? Why do you think I never told you about my grades?"

"Enlighten me?" Joanna dropped onto the sofa,

attempting to light a cigarette.

"Because you're always too drunk to listen. I've failed my A levels and do you know why? Because I don't get any bloody support from you!"

Viv ran up the stairs before her mother had a chance to retaliate.

"What did you say?" she yelled. "You ungrateful little bitch!"

As the last word reverberated off the walls, the wine bottle smashed. Viv slammed the door shut. She needed her father more than any person in the world and punched her bed in utter frustration.

"I miss you, I miss you, I miss you," she cried. "God, please bring my Dad back. Please let me have my Dad back."


David Lancer hadn't returned his friend's motorbike as promised. Instead he was sitting in a burger bar at 10pm pondering the 'twenty pence' girl. Jay's was a popular biker hangout. He decided if his friend wanted the motorbike that much, his powers of elimination would eventually lead him to their regular haunt.

"More coffee David?"

"No thanks, Shirley."

"But your cup's empty?"

"No thanks," he smiled. The chubby waitress was taken aback, no-one ever said 'no' to her coffee.

David took a bite out of a burger he'd been toying with for half an hour. Jay's was situated on a darkened road at the edge of town. Respectable folk would never dream of walking there. He had watched people come and go with bags of greasy unappetising junk food. As he thought about it, he pushed the plate away and looked out of the window, where a familiar shape was drawing close.

"Lancer! So much for bringing her back, eh?"

"What can I say?"

Joe pulled up a seat and with his grubby hands took a monstrous bite out of David's burger.

"What happened to you?" he blurted. "Was it a girl?" he teased.

"I wouldn't call it that. But I'm thinking about one."

"Stop being so bloody mysterious. Where the bloody hell did you get to? Thought you'd had an accident," he said, while licking his fingers.

"Coffee, Joe?"

"You're a gem, Shirley."

Shirley poured while eyeing up David, then shuffled on.

"Think she's got a thing for you my boy."

"I doubt it. I declined her fabulous coffee."

"God, you don't want to do that. Remember what she did to Sean when he said it tasted like tobacco? Poured the bloody lot on his trousers. Women, crazy, the lot of 'em."

David opened his black leather jacket, it cloaked the article he had taken from Viv's table earlier, and pushed it towards Joe.

"Remember him?"

"What, this chap here?"

"Yep. His name is Simon Goddard."

"Never heard of him."

"Look at the picture, you were the one who said you never forget a face."

David watched closely as Joe surveyed the picture.

"Looks familiar. A customer of ours?"

"He was. A good customer as well; never saw so many problems with one car though. I met his daughter this afternoon, at least that's what I've deducted."

"I see."

"Just weird you know, I remember talking to him about his work, my work, his daughter! He showed me a picture of her once. I'm sure it was her at the coffee shop."

"What was she like? Hey, can I get a little service around here?" Joe growled playfully.

"A bit unusual. Very pretty though, but, you know, agitated."

"Aren't we all?"

Shirley shuffled over, folding her last order ready to take the next.

"I gotta go, man."

"See this guy here, Shirley? No manners. He stole my bike and now he's bailing before I've had chance to order. Calls himself a friend?"

"Here," he threw a ten-pound note on the table. "It's on me. See you soon Shirley."

She never even raised an eyebrow. She had fresh meat in front of her and happily took David's seat.

Viv descended the stairs with a heavy heart the next morning. Half-way down the repulsive stench hit her, as it always did on the sixth step. Thankfully, her mother had managed to drag herself to bed but had omitted to clear up her mess. Viv picked up the dustpan as the doorbell chimed.

"Thank God you're home."

Rena walked in a little bleary eyed, and gave Viv a kiss.

"A bit dramatic for a Monday morning don't you think? My Mum's waiting in the car so I'll only be a minute. You look like you need a coffee!"

"Believe me I deserve a cauldron of coffee after the night I've had."

"Oh dear, what has the wicked witch done now?" Rena laughed. It had started off as a joke but now it seemed a little cruel. Rena despised herself for saying it, but she did anyway.

"Look at this mess. Broken bottles, food all over the place. I can't even pretend it was something fun like a party. Mum's getting to be a nightmare. Anyway, enough of this, did you have a nice weekend with your Dad?"

"I don't know yet. I'm still a bit freaked out about what happened last night. Which is why I'm here, but also to see my best friend, of course."

"Obviously," Viv mocked, as she crouched down to sweep up the glass.

"Tonight you're having dinner around my house. Mum's doing your favourite and then I'm going to tell you about what happened."

"Tell me now."

"I can't. I'm off with Mum to an open day. I need to speak to the lecturers about the course I'm starting."

"Oh," Viv replied, a little solemn, as the reality of her situation dawned on her.

"Have you got a free day today?"

"You know I have."

"I have a little task for you. I want you to look up the word Spiritualism, that's all."

"Why?"

"Don't question it, just do it," she smiled as she headed towards the front door. "Oh, by the way, have you told your Mum about your exam results?"

"Have you seen the mess in the living room?"

Rena managed a forced smile. She admired Viv for making light of her problems but it bothered her that she was becoming so blasé about the situation.

"I want you round at 5.30pm prompt. Just remember, Spiritualism."

"I'll remember."


For an English student the absence of a dictionary was a little disconcerting. It was beginning to dawn on her why she hadn't passed her finals. She looked through old piles of books on her shelves but to no avail. There were a couple of thrillers, crime novels and a Thomas the Tank Engine book, which she decided she would read again.

"This is terrible," she uttered. Had she no tangible objects that proved she had attained some level of education? She had passed her GCSEs after all. Her thoughts turned to her father, he had always been a voracious reader and was sure to have a dictionary. She crept quietly out of her bedroom, careful not to wake her mother, and stood directly in front of the spare room. It hadn't been opened in months. The last occupant had been her father, who had slept in the room before he left for America. As she entered, the musty air filled her nose immediately, and she stepped over half-filled boxes to open a small window in the corner of the room. She surveyed the contents of the room. A dusty old mattress leant against the back wall. The boxes contained clothes and books that her father once owned. She knelt down to remember.

'Always pulling faces, weren't you Dad?' she smiled as she picked a photograph off a pile of many. She rummaged through a pile of his books, hoping to find the elusive dictionary.

"Please have one," she said aloud. "Aha! You diamond. I knew there was a boffin in our family."

The dictionary was the most tatty she had ever seen. Nevertheless, she hastily whipped through the pages until she reached the 'sp's'. As the words blended into each other something immediately stood out on the page. Viv sat up and brought the dictionary closer to her face for nearer inspection. A word had been highlighted in a pale blue marker. Someone had highlighted the word Spiritualism. Someone had got there before her.

'This is weird,' she flicked several pages forward and then several pages back, to see if any other words had been highlighted. Suddenly the spare room and all its dusty memories felt uncomfortable, a sharp breeze blew the pale yellow curtains and in doing so re-circulated the dust. Viv leapt up and closed the window, chucked the dictionary back in its box and walked out.

'I'll just tell Rena I don't have a dictionary. She must know that English students are the last people on earth to own dictionaries. Sure, that's what I'll tell her.'

Viv knew that Rena wouldn't fall for that one. She could already visualise the look of disapproval on her face.

It was lucky that Viv's best friend lived only a few feet away. Viv had uncharacteristically drunk a few glasses of wine before dinner. She knew as she crossed Rena's front lawn that it had been a mistake.

'Must walk in a straight line. Must not breathe on Rena's Mum. Must not…' she stopped as she balanced herself on Rena's red front door. She'd walked across the lawn and stamped on one of Carmen's flowers, but decided not to mention it when her friend answered the door. Viv noticed a figure approaching along the hall and slowly moved away so as not to fall.

"Good evening Viv. How are you?"

Viv moved forward. Each action seemed to her to take an awfully long time to carry out.

"I'm fine," she announced and offered a large bar of chocolate in Carmen's direction, which she kindly accepted.

"I'm afraid we didn't have any wine in," letting out a maniacal laugh. She hoped Carmen would get the joke. 'Her mother – the alcoholic? Oh forget it,' she thought and stumbled into the cosy hallway.

"Dinner will be ready in about five minutes. Rena is upstairs. I'll call you girls when it's ready."

Viv turned towards the staircase and smoothed her hand against the red silk material skilfully attached to the wall.

"Rena! I'm coming up the stairs. You better not be naked."

"I'm in my room and I'm not naked."

Viv walked in without knocking, straight into a pile of books.

"Rena, if you had more books, I'd say you were building a library," she said, handing them over. Her friend hadn't moved from her bed where she was sat surrounded by university prospectuses.

"I see you've had a productive day."

"I see you've had a bit to drink."

Viv glanced up, as she was about to take her seat.

"What do you mean?"

"I'm just saying. I can tell when you've had a few."

"How?"

"Your eyes are glazed over. And you have my Mum's marigolds on the bottom of your shoes."

"Shit! Look I'm sorry about your Mum's flowers."

"Are you okay? I'm not saying you have a problem but you've been drinking more than usual, haven't you?"

"I know. I'm just a bit worried about my future. All I want to do is get on with my life and I keep falling back."

"Viv, you've been through a lot. You support your Mum, you always have a smile on your face, I think you're doing great."

"What about my exams? How many more times am I going to fail?"

"A slight technicality. Don't be on a downer, here, catch this. When you pass your exams, this university would be perfect. By the way, did you look up that word I told you to?"

"Sort of," Viv frowned, as she remembered the highlighted page.

"Well, what did you think?"

"I didn't look up the meaning. I think my Mum called for me, so I left it. I'll look it up tomorrow," she replied casually, in the hope that Rena would forget.

"Catch."

Viv caught the flying dictionary before it collided with her face.

"You can look it up now."

"Girls! Dinner is ready."

"Fantastic, I'm hungry." Viv jumped up, "Let's go."

"You're going to look up that word tonight. You're going to need it."


Dinner was a visual feast; extravagant and yet effortlessly done on Carmen's part. There were a variety of curried meats, a prawn dish, a huge bowl of aromatic rice and naan bread. The candlelight and muted lighting added a certain ambience to this Monday night feast.

"I've gone overboard as usual. Maybe you could take some home for your mother?"

Viv handed the rice over to Carmen, while Rena spooned feeble amounts of food onto her plate. As if she needed to lose weight, her curvaceous size 12 frame was enviable.

"Did Rena tell you we went to the university today? Have you started considering where you would like to go?"

Viv smiled, she had to disguise the fact it was the last thing she wanted to do.

"Have you thought about what you would like to do as a career? I remember your mother telling me you're quite the writer. Have you considered journalism?"

"I'm taking a break before university. I don't think I'm talented enough to write, not to your standard anyway."

"Nonsense. You can do anything you want," Carmen said firmly taking a delicate mouthful of food. For the past five years she has been Head of Art at the local grammar school; she also headed up evening classes in creative writing and painting. She was a multi-talented lady. Viv had little confidence in where her own talents lay.

"Rena, you're going to make yourself sick. Slow down, we have all evening."

"Actually, we don't tonight Mum. I'm taking Viv out."

"Where?"

"It's a surprise."

Carmen put her fork down, concerned by the suddenness of the announcement.

"I don't like surprises. I'd like to know where you're going?"

"Mother, I'm twenty-one and have been working for two years to earn money for university. I'm responsible enough not to put myself in any mortal danger."

"I don't care if you're twenty-nine. I want to know

where you're going."

Rena shuffled uncomfortably from side to side and scratched at her neck as if she was being interrogated. Viv shot a worried glance at her friend.

'Oh grief, please don't tell me she's taking me to Alcoholics Anonymous,' Viv thought suddenly.

"Out with it. I want to know where you are going and then I want to enjoy my dinner."

"Very well, we're going to the Spiritualist Church on Elm Drive if you must know."

Viv and Carmen exchanged surprised glances.

"Church? Rena, believe me I'm fine. I'm not looking for God, just yet."

It was a feeble attempt at humour but Viv was trying to say in the nicest possible way – thank you, but no thank you.

"Since when have you been interested in the Spiritualist Church?" Carmen asked coyly. When her daughter was born, Carmen had decided that when she was old enough Rena should decide for herself whether or not to follow a belief.

"I suppose this is your father's influence? Not that I'm against it."

"I just want Viv and me to try something other than the latest cocktail. Is that a crime?" Rena stressed, a bit on the defensive side.

Without batting an eyelid Carmen replied, "Tell me what time the service starts and I'll drop you girls off."

"It starts at 7pm," Rena said a little surprised.

"Carmen, the food was lovely, thank you. I've got to go

though. I promised I'd spend some time with my Mum this evening," Viv stood up.

"Viv, you can't, I've arranged for us to go to this service."

"Well, it's church Rena, we can go some other time."

Viv pushed back her seat and headed for the hallway.

"Thank you for the chocolate dear," Carmen added.

Once they were out of the dining room Rena cornered Viv on her way out.

"It's important that you come tonight."

"I've never been to church. Why do you want me to come?"

"It isn't quite the same as Sunday mass, let's put it that way. I just want you to see what I saw, it's quite an experience. If you're determined not to come now just think it over. It's the Spiritualist Church on Elm Drive."


"You're back early."

"I wasn't hungry."

Viv perched herself on the edge of a chair and watched her mother as she lit up.

"I have news." Joanna brightened.

Viv flicked her hair as she always did when she was out of sorts.

"I received a call from a friend of mine this evening. She's leaving her current job and has managed to get an interview for me to replace her. How about that?"

"That's great. What will you be doing?"

"Mainly reception work, manning the switchboard, greeting clients, that sort of thing. That's if I get it of course," she said nervously. Viv expected her mother to go on and on, but she stopped silent, staring down at the floor as she finished her cigarette.

"Is there anything else? You look as though you have something on your mind."

"I've arranged for you to see a counsellor tomorrow morning."

"I suppose the reception job was a way of easing in, huh?"

"It will be for your own good. I'm useless at the moment. I think these exam results are a cry for help."

"If it will make you happier, then sure. I'll try anything once, apart from hard drugs."

Viv surprised herself how 'matter of fact' she took the news.

"I'm sorry about last night. I didn't mean what I said. I think you've coped amazingly well. I know you're capable of doing anything you want to. At the same time I think it will be a good idea for you to speak to Doctor Cross. You need to put the last year into perspective so we can look to the future."

"Sounds good Mum." She could see how much her mother was trying for her.

"Fancy a video night? How about a bit of John Wayne? Remember how you loved his films when you were little?"

"I can't tonight Mum. I'm going out with Rena." Viv knew that curiosity would eventually get the better of her.

"Where are you headed?"

"This is going to sound a little strange, but to the Spiritualist Church on Elm Drive."

Joanna froze. Ash decorated the carpet from her newly lit cigarette.

"What did you say? Spiritualist Church?"

"Yes. This horrifies you more than the thought of me getting plastered?"

Joanna stubbed out the cigarette and walked over to her daughter.

"You are never to go near a Spiritualist Church. Do you hear?" Joanna grabbed at Viv's arm. Viv stepped back and as she did, her mother's arms flopped to her side.

Her body looked limp and weak but her voice had conviction. She wondered what had stirred in her to provoke such a reaction. It was only church for crying out loud!

"Rena obviously has an interest and I'm going along to find out what it's about."

"Stay here with me. We can open a bottle of wine, order a pizza…"

"No, I can't. I promised her, sort of. It's a church service so it probably won't be any longer than…"

"I'm asking you not to go Vivien."

"Mum have you been sipping the loony juice again? This is a church. Have you been to this one before?"

Taken aback, Joanna stuttered before answering.

"Why would you say that?"

"I found something today, in the spare bedroom, amongst Dad's old books."

"It's not a good idea to go in there. There are too many memories."

"The point is, I was looking for a dictionary, attempting

to find out what the word Spiritualism actually means. The word and the meaning were highlighted."

"Well, I don't know anything about that," she said unconvincingly, as she sat back on the sofa. "Baby, I just don't want you getting into any weird cult thing. So please stay away."

Viv knew her mother got upset over just about anything, whether it was exams or an over-priced bottle of wine. This church thing should have been no different, but there was something about the way her mother was pleading that made her worried. It did the opposite of scaring her off, now she wanted to go to the church and find out for herself.

"Mum, just relax. I'll go out and get you a packet of twenty and then I'll be back."

"Since when do you buy my cigarettes? You're the one who keeps telling me to quit. It's just an excuse to go to that church." And it was. Joanna padded over to the fridge and took out a bottle of wine.

"I guess it's another evening alone," she announced.

◆

ELM DRIVE was an unassuming little street just left of a row of moderately busy shops and public houses. The street was jammed with cars. Luckily, Viv had been wise enough to take a taxi. She had been drinking earlier and didn't want to take a chance. She darted into the church, conscious that she was minutes late.

As she pushed the heavy wooden doors open, she

could hear the service had already started. The congregation, which consisted of about eighty people, were standing and singing. She fixed on one particular face and wondered how long he could hold that last note. The old woman at the piano kept her fingers pressed firmly on the keys, as the congregation took their seats. Viv put a firm hand to her lips to stop herself from laughing. 'Gullible fools', she thought. What sort of salvation could be found in Ossilton anyway?

"Would you like to take a seat? There is room at the back."

Viv whipped round and squinted at the man stood on the stage. She could barely make out his features.

"Yes, thank you," she could hardly say no. She spotted Rena who looked thrilled to see her friend. Viv promptly took the seat next to Rena and hoped the curious looks would die down.

"Is this your first visit to the Spiritualist Church?"

If Viv hadn't become engrossed at the sight of the bric-a-brac stall she would have answered the question. There was some impressively priced junk adorning the makeshift table. An orange Sixties-style vase for only seventy pence!

"Miss, the question's for you," the lady sitting behind prodded her. She looked towards the vicar or priest, or whatever he was, and tried once more to make him out. At least fifty, with an impressive mop of black hair, his mouldy green jumper made him look much older than his years.

"Yes, it is," she answered quickly, in the hope he

would begin the service.

"Tonight is a very special evening for us all. Our Medium comes all the way from the sunny Californian coast, although he now calls England his home."

The congregation put their hands together enthusiastically as he entered from a side door.

"Viv."

Viv couldn't quite make out the man, who was now in polite conversation with the jumper.

"Viv!" Rena finally got a word in as the clapping ebbed away. "Thanks for coming."

"I was curious, plus I had wondered if it had something to do with the stories my Dad told me when I was little."

"What stories?"

"Shush, it's about to start."

Rena handed Viv a pair of glasses. She could see her friend desperately trying to focus on the man who had just taken centre stage. Viv's drunken haze had yet to clear.

"Wear these. I find I don't need them any more."

Viv scrambled to put them on and felt her face drop in disbelief as his face came clearly into focus.

"Thanks for your warm reception. I've been a little rusty lately so forgive me if I'm not quite on target."

"He's so cute!" Rena gushed. "I hope he comes to me tonight," Rena cooed. Viv turned to witness a show of adulation she had not yet seen in her usually practical friend. But it wasn't her friend's enthusiasm that had perturbed her, it was the man up on stage. It was the man from the coffee shop! She hid her face with her hand and slowly slumped down into her seat, hoping not to be noticed.

"Wonder how old he is?" Rena whispered, as her breath caught in her chest. The Medium closed his eyes in concentration. The hall fell silent with expectant anticipation. Even Viv moved her hand away from her face to see what he would do next.

"I would like to come to the gentleman in the black jumper in the second row. Good evening, sir."

"Good evening," the man replied, bolt upright in his chair.

Viv couldn't quite believe that the person before her was a 'church-going' man. His clothes suggested otherwise. His leather jacket and scuffed boots indicated he would be more at home at a bikers' convention than a house of worship.

"I hoped he would choose me," Rena whispered.

Viv wasn't listening.

"Could you tell me if you have a grandmother in Spirit?"

"Yes I have," the man replied hopefully.

"I have a large woman with me, extremely opinionated but very caring. She says, "Ask him about pickled onions.""

The man made a sound reminiscent of an excited puppy. His round jowls quivered with delight.

"Does this sound like your grandmother on your mother's side?" he enquired gently.

"Grandma's pickled onions were amazing. She used to make them for me."

"What is going on Rena?"

"Just listen."

David moved closer as if he was planning to confide some secret information. The entire congregation fixated on every word.

"She wants to know why you have given up? She told you that you should never give in, even when things are tough. Does this make sense to you?"

The man lowered his gaze. The initial excitement drained visibly from his face.

"Yes, it does. My wife left me four months ago."

"Do not despair, she tells me. The black cloud that has been hanging over your life will move during the next few months; you will be feeling better. Your grandmother wants to tell you that you are stronger than this. She is leaving me now, but watches over you, all of the time. God bless."

David took a moment to compose himself, taking a sip of water from his glass.

"That poor man. Is this legal?"

"Viv, for an intelligent girl you do come out with some silly questions."

David surveyed his eager audience. Viv panicked momentarily as he began to focus where she was sitting. Luckily he hadn't noticed Viv's presence, his attention directed towards a fragile looking blonde, no older than she.

"Good evening, miss."

"Good evening," she replied a little unsure.

"I have two women who would like to talk to you. The vibration suggests that they are your aunts and from your father's side."

She looked up, slightly confused, then familiarity spread across her face as she remembered.

"Yes, they died before I was born. I know I had an Aunt Aggie but I can't remember the other's name," she spoke nervously.

"They're glad you found the china doll."

For a moment, the congregation fell completely silent. You could hear a pin drop. The girl didn't move a muscle, dumbfounded by the precision of his words; uncertain what to say next.

"They understand you feel emotionally shattered. A special relationship has come to an end and it may feel as though happiness will never happen again. Does that make sense to you?"

"Yes it does," she replied, "thank you."

"Keep focused on where you want to be in life. That's all they wanted to convey to you, God bless."

It was a surreal moment for Viv who wriggled uncomfortably in her seat.

"Have you got worms or something?"

"No, I'm fine. It's just weird that's all. How does he know all this stuff?"

Though her father had talked of angels watching over people, she had, at the time, taken it as pure fantasy. It never occurred to her that the stories could have a ring of truth about them. Viv watched as his eyes swept over her row stopping abruptly on herself.

"Good evening, may I come to you?"

Viv didn't know what to say.

"Viv, say yes," Rena strained, through her clenched teeth.

"Who wants to know?" erupted from her mouth, unaware that Rena had pinched her arm. David sniggered and brushed back his hair as he waited. At that moment, something clicked inside him. The young woman before him was familiar, the events of the previous day came tumbling back.

"Viv, say something."

"If you feel uncomfortable about a message from Spirit, it's not a problem," his kindly eyes lingered on Viv in the hope that she had remembered him.

"Hello," she replied at last, "Do you have a message for me?"

"Well done," Rena whispered.

"I have an older woman, a grandmother figure. She is telling me that you are at an important time in your life. The difficulties you are experiencing now are important to your journey. You can expect to travel in the very near future."

"Does she say when?"

"She won't give me an exact date. It really will be up to you."

"Travel?" Viv mumbled, she didn't even have a job. Her mother had once told her that education was the passport to anywhere she wanted to go. Her only prospect of travel was a trip to the local job centre. For a moment she wondered if he had got his wires crossed but she smiled nevertheless.

"Is anyone else with you?"

"No miss. I'm afraid the lady has left me now. So I'll say good night and God bless to you."

Viv made a swift exit when the service came to a close some thirty minutes later. Rena was fast on her tail, curiosity had been killing her.

"Do you know this guy?" Rena gushed. "He kept smiling at you."

"Sort of. I met him in a coffee shop. He gave me twenty pence."

"So you've been flirting?"

"I'd hardly call talking to a stranger, flirting."

"Viv, aren't you excited? You got a reading."

"Sure I'm pleased, I'd rather it had been from someone else."

"I know," Rena replied quietly. "I'm glad you came. It gives you a new perspective on things doesn't it?"

"What does?"

"The fact that nobody dies. The people we love, are here, all around, watching us. Do you believe?"

Viv smiled back at her friend and embraced her lightly, she wasn't sure what to believe, but she was thankful she had come that evening.

"Come in and meet the congregation. I want to introduce myself," Rena pleaded.

"Not tonight, I want to get home. You go back inside."

"Will you tell me what you thought of tonight?"

"Tomorrow when it's sunk in, I'll give you an answer. I agree, it was interesting. Goodnight sweetie."

To her annoyance, Viv could not get a taxi and walking alone at night wasn't the most comforting of prospects. As she made the journey along Spencer Street, the familiar sights of shops and run-down kebab houses lent a false sense of security as she felt the brightness envelop her.

"Get yourself in this car right now, Vivien!" Joanna yelled from her half lowered window.

"Have you been spying on me?"

"What on earth are you doing walking along Spencer Street at this hour?"

"I couldn't get a taxi. The number was constantly busy."

Viv dropped in beside her mother, somewhat annoyed but rather relieved. They drove along in silence for a moment. Viv cringed as her mother began to light up.

It was filthy habit and wished she would give it up.

"How long have you been waiting for me?"

"About fifteen minutes," she puffed through a cloud of smoke.

"You know, you shouldn't be driving Mum."

"I haven't had a drink this evening. I was tempted but I decided not to."

"That's really good."

"So, tell me what happened this evening?"

Viv was still curious to know why her mother had got a bee in her bonnet over a church.

"It was a simple service. The only difference is that a Spiritualist Medium presides over the evening."

"And?"

"Nothing happened. They tried to pass a message to me but I said no." It was a lie but a white one. The truth would only make her mother upset.

"That's good. They're nuts baby. You won't have to go there again."

"Why are you so against it anyway?"

"Let's just get home. Remember you have your appointment tomorrow."

"How could I forget? You'll have me in a strait-jacket next."

Joanna sighed deeply, exhaling a long stream of smoke and pursing her lips together tightly. For all their bickering, she was glad Viv was safe.

◆

JOANNA HAD spared no expense. The plush doctor's waiting room, adorned with original works of art, felt more like the lobby of a luxurious hotel.

"You can thank your father for this."

"Don't say that."

"Well, it's true," her voice deliberately raised attracted the attention of the lady sitting opposite.

"I thought these places were supposed to be filled with…" Viv gave her mother a knowing glance.

"With what?" she replied innocently.

"Nutters! People talking gibberish to themselves. People who smell at the very least."

"Viv!"

"All I see is posh people smelling of Chanel."

"Do you smell?" Joanna quipped.

"No, I had a bath this morning."

"Do you talk gibberish?"

"Okay, I get your point," Viv stressed, raising her voice so the pearly-clad woman was once again distracted.

"So, when do I go in?"

"Anytime now. She's a very nice lady so I would appreciate you not saying 'bloody' in her presence."

"How do you know she's nice?"

"She's a doctor isn't she?"

The mahogany door clicked opened and a pretty young woman with a severe black fringe appeared.

"Miss Goddard, Doctor Cross will see you now."

Viv stood up and waited for her mother to do the same.

"You're coming with me aren't you? I mean my problems and your problems are kind of the same thing, right?"

"No, I'll wait for you here. It's just you and Doctor Cross."

It was probably for the best. After all, she couldn't talk to her mother about last night. Viv was contemplating asking what were the doctor's views on Spiritualism.

Viv already had a preconceived idea of how a psychiatrist's office should look. The back wall (the one which the patient notices first) should be filled with various certificates, ranging from diplomas to the prestigious doctorate, all mounted in elegant silver frames. At the far end, a grand bookcase would house evidence of the doctor's notable intellect, which the patient would occasionally glance at, when they ran out of words to say. That in her opinion, was the mark of a real doctor. Viv was not disappointed with the reality.

"Good morning, Vivien. My name is Abigail Cross. How do you do?" extending a hand laden with diamonds.

"Hello."

"Do you prefer Viv or Vivien?"

"Usually people call me Viv, apart from my Mum."

"Then I'll call you Viv. Please take a seat."

She did so, while eyeing up the chaise longue on the other side of the room. As Doctor Cross shuffled with papers Viv could see her extensive qualifications. It took Viv back to her collection which consisted of six GCSEs, a cycling proficiency when she was nine and a Blue Peter badge.

"I presume you're college-bound in the next month or so? You look about the same age as my daughter. Though she opted not to carry on her education."

Viv sat up, this cheered her suddenly.

"Why not?"

"She's never been an academic. Rosie is very artistic. She's taken a gap year in France and wants to become a writer."

"I love writing."

"Have you ever thought about a career in that field?" she enquired.

"Yes but I don't want to go to university."

"What area would you like to go into?"

"I like writing stories, but I'm not hard-nosed enough to go into journalism." Viv laughed nervously.

"How did you feel about coming here today?"

"I didn't really feel anything. I was up for it. I can see why my Mum made the appointment. She totally flipped when she found out I had failed my A Levels again."

Doctor Cross smiled knowingly, as if she had been through the process herself. Most probably with Rosie. Viv couldn't help staring at the meticulously turned out Doctor Cross. Her blonde curly hair was cut just above her shoulders and her attractive face painted with care and attention. She was a more expensive version of her mother and a nicer smelling one too.

"Well that's a completely natural reaction, she wants you to do well. I'm sure you'd be a little disappointed if she didn't make a fuss."

Viv thought for a moment and imagined if her mother had simply ignored her results.

"I know Mum cares. I just wish she wouldn't lose her temper. What do you suggest I do?"

"You need to let your Mum know how much her temper upsets you. Why do you think she is easily angered?"

Viv took a sharp intake of breath and wondered where to start.

"Because I've totally messed up my exams, and to be truthful I don't really want to carry on my education, not right now anyway."

"Well that's the beauty of further education, you can pick up where you left off at any time in your life."

"Try telling that to my Mum, she thinks the world begins and ends with a degree. What makes matters worse is that I've told her I'll go to university after I've taken the resits."

"It's always best to say exactly how you feel and explain to your Mum what you want, not what she wants to hear."

"I'll be alright. I've been wallowing in self-pity for too long and it's getting a little tiring for Mum and myself. I think I've made a mini-breakthrough, something quite unusual happened last night, something I'd like to learn more about."

"Would you like to talk about it?"

"Do you believe in Spirits, Doctor Cross?"

"Life after death?"

"Yes."

"I do as a matter of fact."

"I think I experienced that last night. I went to the Spiritualist Church in Elm Drive and had a reading. The Medium told me my grandmother wanted to contact me. It gave me hope that maybe this rut I'm in is for a reason and that I'm about to get out."

"What else did she communicate to you?"

"That I'm about to travel."

"That sounds wonderful."

"Do you think it sounds a little hokey? I only ask because my Mum wants nothing to do with it."

"The unknown can be hard for people to digest. You're expressing a healthy interest and have every right to question the afterlife. It is something that is well-documented by professionals, and people who have had first-hand experience."

"I feel better already," Viv grinned.

Maybe therapy was just an opportunity to blurt out all those nagging questions. If that was true, her main one had been answered. In Viv's eyes, her rehabilitation was finished.

"That was quick. Is everything alright?" Joanna shot a concerned look at Doctor Cross.

"Absolutely fine, Mrs Goddard. Viv is free to come back any time she wishes to. She's been a pleasure."

Abigail closed the mahogany door behind her, leaving only Viv and her mother in the waiting room.

"I've paid for the entire hour. You've been in there only ten minutes. What happened? Didn't you like her?"

"I'll tell you on the way home." Viv felt uncharacteristically elated.

◆

CARMEN NEVER had accidents. She had always been proud of the fact they she had not had an accident in twenty-one years of driving. In this case, it wasn't her fault. She had parked outside the local art supplier. As she was carefully reversing she was sure the car coming in her direction would wait, but it only picked up speed and hit her side on. Luckily no-one was injured but Carmen felt more of a dent in her pride, considering her record was impeccable. Better than any man she knew.

"David, I hope you can work your magic. A reckless young man did this, if only there were more careful drivers around like you."

"You've never seen me driving!"

"The only good thing that has come out of this horrible situation is that I've got together with one of my former pupils. How have you been, dear?" she wiped a bead of sweat from her forehead. The afternoon air was still and humid and she gladly accepted the offer of a cold beer. David walked round the side of the car while Carmen sat on a deck chair, enjoying the contents from David's on-site fridge.

"Good actually. Saving up for a new bike."

"Oh no, too dangerous. You'd be better off sticking with an engine on four wheels. But then, who am I to talk? I hope you have continued with your art?"

"Well, it turns out that art doesn't pay well. So I continued to do the thing I've always done, fixing cars and fixing motorbikes."

Carmen put down her can of beer on the worn grass below her feet and folded her arms as if she were about to give a severe warning to an unruly student.

"Art doesn't pay well? Art doesn't begin and end with a canvas and a paintbrush. There are so many things you can do nowadays."

"I know that but…"

"But what?"

"You're right, but this is what I do now," he shrugged.

"I know dear and you do it very well," she said admiringly, as she surveyed what he had built up. Although he worked out of the garage adjoining his house, he had one of the best reputations in the area.

"So," she began, indicating a change of subject. "How

are things in your personal life, if you don't mind my intrusion?"

"Carmen," he sighed. "I have a closer relationship with this bike than any woman right now."

"I'm sure you're being modest. In fact, I hear through acquaintances you're quite the favourite at the church you attend."

David, accidentally spitting out his drink, looked startled.

"How do you know about my church?"

"I'm on the committee with the local council, we know everything," she said proudly. "It just came to me," she said sitting upright. "My daughter attended the Spiritualist Church last night."

"What is her name?"

"Rena."

"I left the service as soon as it ended, so I wouldn't have seen her. If she decides to attend again. I'd love to meet her."

"Remember that painting you gave me?"

"Do you mean that pathetic thank-you gift I forced upon you."

"It's the most lovely painting I have David."

"What about it?" he wondered, taking another swig from his can.

"I went there once on holiday."

David put down his can and looked curiously at his former teacher.

"Carmen, that painting came from my imagination. It's not a scene I copied from a book or a place from a childhood holiday," he smiled quietly.

"The flowers you painted, the details in the rock formations, the sky you envisaged was exactly how I remember that beach. You would have been amazed. Maybe you're destined to go there."

"Maybe," he warmed to the possibility.

"I'll be back in two days to pick the car up. Thank you again, David."

"Can I get you a taxi?"

"No, no. It's a beautiful afternoon and I haven't had a nice walk in ages."


"I liked Doctor Cross, a lot. She was great, very un-doctor like."

"So why did you leave so soon? I mean . . ," she paused, "All that money and nothing. I hope you told her about your exam failure."

"Gee, thanks Mum."

"I didn't mean it like that."

"Why can't you understand that I need time to find out what I want?"

"That's why I booked an appointment now, because there is no time. Because the nosy bitch over there is constantly asking what bloody university you're going to."

"Don't speak about Carmen like that."

"Well that daughter of hers certainly is. I watch her when she comes over here. Looking down on us as if we've got six heads."

Seeing her mother this animated was extremely

disconcerting. Viv hid her irritation under a large mug of steaming coffee.

"I know she's your best friend and you've known her since the age of four, blah, blah… but she's smug and probably intent on discouraging you from going to university just to make herself feel more proud."

"That's not true," Viv fiercely intervened. "In fact, she's the one person who's trying to encourage me. It was her idea to go to the church and try something new."

"Some friend. Introducing you to a load of nonsense."

"Why do you say that?" Viv asked exasperated.

"Nothing, nothing. I'm going for a bath."

Joanna simply couldn't let Viv go. She was frightened to let her make her own decisions and make her own mistakes. In many ways Joanna was frightened of life and refused to believe that her daughter could make a success on her own. At the same time Viv felt vulnerable, almost twenty-two and yet to realise what to do with her own life. She hoped her grandmother's surprise intervention was a sign that the difficult period had finally come to a close and brighter things were in store for her future.

## Flashback

*"Dad?"*

*Viv stared at the clock ahead, it was 4am. A damp hand brushed through her hair; it was her own. It was still dark outside. She checked herself, touched her chest, her face, making sure she was still Viv Goddard and she was. She searched for her slippers with her feet and walked over to the same pink-rimmed mirror she had had since she was a child. She wondered what time it must be in California and what her Dad was doing and if he was thinking about her.*

*"On the beach, somewhere hot, I'm sure. You love the sea, don't you Dad?" she whispered softly as she touched his picture, steadying it, as it threatened to fall out of the frame. She moved closer to the mirror and inspected her drawn face. Her eyes hovered over her room and watched her own reflection, fast asleep on the bed.*

*"That's me," she sighed heavily, "Asleep, peaceful and unaware of my Dad's accident. But that's all about to change."*

## Presently

VIV PUSHED her coffee aside and shook her head vigorously, hoping that would take away the pain of that silly dream.

"It meant nothing," she said forcefully.

The doorbell rang out.

"Vivien. Get the door. I'm in the bath!"

Viv ignored her mother. She would have to answer the door even if she wasn't in the bath. She already knew who it would be, no-one else ever knocked for them.

"Hey Viv, feel like talking about last night?"

"Sure, come in."

Rena moved excitedly towards the sofa and waited patiently for her friend to follow.

"Rena, are you alright?"

"I just want to know what you thought about the church. I also have some very exciting news."

"Tell me then."

"No, you first."

"Okay, I do believe that there is something out there. It just seems too fantastic at the moment. My Mum thinks it's all a load of nonsense," Viv said.

"My Dad took me to his church last weekend. I didn't get a reading but the things the Medium knew were just incredible. This one lady, he told her that her grandfather was glad she found his old Monopoly board in the attic. I mean, how would he know she was in the attic?"

Viv couldn't help but grin, her friend was in the most spirited state. She seemed to have been converted in only two visits.

"I am interested to find out more, but I want to hear your news, Rena."

"It all happened this morning. My Mum had a little accident in the car, a small bump but she is alright. To make a potentially long story short, she took her car to the local mechanic who turns out to be one of her past art students. You'll never guess who he is?"

"Who?"

"David Lancer. The Medium at the Spiritualist Church last night. Now if that's not a coincidence I don't know what is."

This revelation brought a smile to Viv's face, the first genuine smile in a long time, even Rena couldn't hide her pleasure on this monumental occasion.

"You like him!" Rena ventured mischievously. "You love him."

"Oh get off. You're crazy."

In one swift movement Viv got up from the sofa and made her way over to the kettle.

"You can't change the subject by walking away, I know you too well. I was going to let it slip but I have to tell you; your face was a picture when you first laid eyes on David, you went as red as a beetroot. I saw you, hiding your face with your hand. I know all your tricks Vivien Goddard, admit it, you like him."

"No, I don't."

"If I know anything about you and men it's that you make a complete fool of yourself over the ones you like most. You're the most un-cool girl, I know."

"Thanks Rena."

"I mean with men, potential love interests."

"And you're any better? Remember Andrew Davies, the sweet guy who brought you flowers all the time. You broke up with him because you said he distracted you from your homework, and you call me un-cool."

"Okay, so we're both hopeless with men. Do I get a coffee too?"

"No," she replied, in a petulant tone. Rena reached for her own mug and made her own drink.

"You're invited to dinner tonight."

"It's very nice of you but we do have food. I admit we do have more wine bottles than most households, but we do eat solids occasionally."

"Okay smart ass, I was just asking. You know how my

Mum loves to cook, any excuse. Another thing I forgot to mention…"

"Yes?"

"David is invited also."

"The guy we've just been talking about? How? Why?"

"Why are you so interested all of a sudden?" Rena said nonchalantly, as she took her mug over to the kitchen table.

"I'm not. I didn't know your Mum and him were that close?"

"They're getting re-acquainted. He was an art student at one of Mum's evening classes. Apparently he has family over here, that's why he made the move from the States. He's the perfect age too, twenty-nine, not too old and not too young. I'm so glad she phoned him this afternoon and invited him over."

"So, what time is he arriving?"

"Well, it's not really of interest to someone who has plenty of food stocked in the fridge and doesn't fancy him anyway. It would simply be a waste of an evening."

"No, I don't care," she convinced herself. "You have a nice night."

Rena shook her head in disbelief.

"You like him, admit it."

It was 10pm and Viv was experiencing her first taste of the spy game. She was perched, not so comfortably, on the window ledge in her darkened hallway, cloaked by the heavy curtains. Binoculars verged on the crazy but she needed a clearer focus, in the hope she would see

Carmen's new guest. Her mother had nodded-off hours ago after a very long bath.

'I have no life, do I?' she questioned herself, while trying to fight the cramp in her leg. She had been concentrating on his motorbike for some time, so she was sure he was in the house tucking into one of Carmen's specialities. As he was a special guest she would probably do desserts. She should have accepted the invitation.

"This is so pathetic. If Rena could see me now she'd have me sectioned."

Viv finally reasoned that a night in front of the television, was better than a night sat aimlessly on a window ledge. She flopped onto the sofa and pressed standby. A moment later, the doorbell rang. She had two choices, number one would be to answer the door and in doing so reveal a gigantic sweet and sour spattering on her white jumper. Number two would be to sneak out into the back garden, and indulge in a little late night weeding, the doorbell surely wouldn't be audible from that distance. Realising the latter was about as likely as a visit from the Queen, she proceeded to the door.

"Hi, he's with me. Be nice."

"He can't come in. I've spilt sauce everywhere and I look a mess."

"So? He's only come over to say hello. We've been talking about you over dinner. So be nice, invite him in."

Viv peered outside to no avail. She stepped onto the porch to find a dark looking figure hovering by her car.

"Nice little beast this. Yours?"

"Yes, my Dad bought it for me."

"I know," he said calmly. His gentle American cadence was so different and exciting to her senses. He was some exotic creature who had descended on Willow Court that night. He walked closer to Viv so that his face was illuminated by the outside light. His black hair was enviably shiny and his dark brown eyes seemed unusually gentle, not quite a man's, yet not in the least bit feminine. He was a wonder for a single female who hadn't had a boyfriend since…

"How did you know my Dad bought me this car?" Viv questioned in earnest, dropping the school-girl crush act. "Oh wait a minute," she stopped dead, as she turned to go into the house, "My grandma told you?"

The delayed response was strange enough but to her surprise he had disappeared out of sight. For a moment she found the entire situation rather humorous. "Is he an illusionist too?" Losing her best friend's special guest in the space of ninety seconds had to be a world record.

"What are you two doing out here?" Rena appeared at the door.

"He's gone. One minute we're talking and then abracadabra boom! Like magic."

Viv chuckled.

"Very funny. Where did he go? I told you to be polite to him."

"I was. Perhaps he's under the car Rena." Viv mused.

Rena examined the car's undercarriage when the unmistakable sound of a motorbike revved to the limit offended their ears.

"Ladies!"

"Where did you disappear to?"

David sat comfortably on his motorbike as if the conversation had never happened.

"Like a ride?"

"Would I? No way, you might never bring me back." Viv walked cautiously nearer.

"Possibly."

The opportunity of doing something scary sent a tingle up her spine. Carmen appeared in the doorway and beckoned Rena in.

"I presume you've met David, Viv?"

"Not properly. Is he safe?"

"In what respect?" she chuckled.

"He wants me to take a ride on his bike. Will he bring me back?"

"I'm sure he will. Have a go."

"I don't know," Viv trailed.

Rena joined her mother, looked cuttingly in the direction of her friend and walked back inside the house.

"Another time maybe."

"It's my clumsy way of introducing myself. I love riding bikes, I'm as safe as houses plus my name is David. Carmen was once my art teacher, I gave you a twenty pence piece and I saw you at the church last night. Plus, I love Homer Simpson!"

It was the fear of falling off the bike and her legs being torn to shreds, which worried her most. Had he presented her with a vehicle with a minimum of three wheels she wouldn't have been standing there at all.

"Would you tell me how you know my Dad bought

me my car?"

"If you come out on the bike, I might tell you."

His quiet desperation endeared Viv to act completely out of character. Instead of shrinking away, she took a chance, and allowed herself to be helped onto the bike.

Without a blink of an eye she accepted the second helmet and shoved it hard onto her head. Viv made herself comfortable on the seat. It was far wider than she had expected. She held onto the bar behind with all her might and prayed they were only going to circle the block. His hero, after all, was Homer Simpson!

Viv only knew bikers as fictitious characters in films. She had a vision of bulging muscles, leathers and tattoos. David headed out of town, Viv knew the general direction but had never stopped at the roadside café before. Her heart sank at the sight of her evening venue – dirty bikes, unwashed windows, torn cola signs – but there was something friendly about the place. The bikers were accepting of strangers. She felt like an outsider looking in. Jay's café felt nice.

"Would you like something to eat?" he offered.

"My dinner's on my jumper."

It had meant to be an icebreaker; a joke, to make this unusual situation feel more comfortable, instead he smiled, and looked at the greasy menu. The restaurant was starkly lit. Viv was conscious that the plump waitress in the corner was eyeing her up.

"Do you like cola?"

"That's fine."

They sat in a window booth with a panoramic view of the car park.

"Are these your friends?"

"They're people I know, yeah. I wouldn't call them friends, well, not close friends."

Viv sneaked a look at her reflection, conscious of the sauce stain which seemed to have doubled in size.

"Why did you want me to come on the bike with you?" It seemed the obvious question to ask.

"Because I wanted to tell you about the car."

Viv put down the salt shaker she was nervously playing with.

"It used to be mine, I sold it to your Dad."

"I knew it must have been something like that."

"I'm very sorry about your father. He was a good man."

"Thanks."

At that moment Shirley made her way over to the table, knocking Viv hard on the shoulder.

"I'm sorry," she whined, "It's a slow night, I'm falling asleep over there. Would you like something to eat?"

"Two colas, Shirley," David replied, his focus still fixed on Viv. "I read about it in the local paper. He used to come to me to get his car fixed."

"He died over a year ago, an accident, while he was overseas on business."

"You know, he talked about you a lot."

"Oh my gosh, what did he say?" she perked up suddenly.

"Well, let me see. He mentioned your driving. Saying you're a little wild when you get behind the wheel…"

"Go on," she sat back.

"You're not the greatest cook but you make the best cheese on toast."

"He knows I'm a terrible cook…"

"You make the best coffee even though it's his least favourite drink."

"What else?" she breathed deeply, as if this flash of dialogue had eased the pain of the last year. Her father was coming back in these small insignificant details.

"He misses you."

"He misses me? He told you that when he was getting his brakes fixed? I didn't think my Dad was that sentimental." She smiled, never realising what that last connotation suggested, until she caught David's eye, and something suddenly became clear.

"He misses me? You're talking to him now?"

Shirley made her way over, spilling most of Viv's cola on the table and then shuffled on.

"Would you throw that drink in my face if I told you he was?"

"Of course not," she smiled. "I'd be shocked though. Are you talking to him?"

"Yes, your Dad often comes to me."

Her heart was now beating faster than it ever had before, she had to stay calm and quickly asked another question.

"What does it mean to channel?"

"You want me to explain it to you now?"

"Sure."

"It's a relaxed state. Channelling simply means

clearing your mind and allowing Spirit to contact you, whether they choose to talk or appear to you. When I channel I empty my mind, or as much as I possibly can."

"And you can hear them?"

"I can hear them. We call it being clairaudient."

"What is my Dad saying?" she enquired nervously.

"The voice isn't clear, there are other Spirits who are also trying to be heard. But I can tell you this, he's very pleased we have met."

This startling information was of great comfort to Viv, though she didn't want to hear any more.

"Thank you David, that means a lot."

"Perhaps I can teach you to channel?"

"My Mum wouldn't be happy about that. She'd make my life a living hell."

"Mums are like that," he chuckled, "Now, I better get you home Viv."

"I've really enjoyed this conversation David, I'm pleased I've met you."

"Me too."

They ventured out into the cold night, though Viv didn't feel it.

"Your carriage awaits!"

David handed Viv her helmet. She braced herself for the journey home as he turned the key.

"David, I don't know much about bikes but that doesn't sound very good."

"Yeah I know. Do you mind if you hop off? I'll need to take a look at it. You go back inside."

"No, I'm alright. It's refreshing out here."

Viv wandered along the stony driveway. Her head tilted back, she searched aimlessly for Orion's belt. Her father had once told her how to find it.

"Are you okay over there? This might take a while."

"I'm alright. Just finding Orion's belt," she called over.

She became slightly dizzy after a while, and found herself wandering away from the restaurant and along the country lane. It was so peaceful, so still. The stars seemed to be winking at her. She wondered if her father might be looking on at that very moment. She felt safe ambling along, with only a thought of her handsome knight.

"Viv, I think this beast is ready to roll. Viv?" David turned around; Viv had disappeared out of sight. He glanced into the restaurant but she hadn't sneaked back in. The gravel crunched underfoot as he looked down the lane.

"Hey Viv?"

He stood in the middle of the lane, searching in both directions. He couldn't see her, there wasn't a response.

"Come on Viv!"

Something wasn't right. David walked down the road, his pace quickened.

"Viv!" he yelled, pounding the road towards the shape in the distance. She turned towards the source of his voice, but the angry sound of tyres on the country road turned her once again. She froze that instant, the high beam blinded her, and she knew instantly that something was going to hit her.

Two cold hands gripped her shoulders firmly, and with a

force likened to an express train, her body flew, hitting the side of the grass bank like a rag doll. All she could feel was the warm trickling sensation of blood in her mouth. It made her want to gag. Hazy voices and panic encompassed her. Heavy breathing invaded her face. She had only felt this sensation once before at her father's funeral, when everyone was mindlessly asking, *"Are you alright?"*

"Viv? Open your eyes! Viv!" the voice repeated, echoing inside her head.

The figures hadn't come into focus and they wouldn't leave her alone. The pain was fast becoming unbearable, and she began to scream.

"I'll call an ambulance!" a voice cried out.

"I don't understand it! She was stood there one minute and the next she was at the side of the road." The guy who had been driving crouched down and placed two trembling hands on his temples, trying to work out how it had happened.

"Was I speeding?" he panicked, shaking so that he fell back onto his car, now at a stand-still in the centre of the lane.

"Don't worry," David glanced back. He was having little luck getting Viv to focus.

"An ambulance is on its way. Is she breathing?"

"She's breathing, her eyes are half open which is a good sign."

"Should we move her?" the woman offered, moving nervously back and forth.

"I don't think so. Have you got a blanket?"

"Yes, in the boot," she brightened at the thought of being able to help, ignoring her partner who was crying uncontrollably in the road.

David put the blanket under her head and wrapped his thick heavy jacket around her shoulders. He wiped her bloodied mouth gently.

"Viv this is David. Do you know who I am?"

The tears tumbled and if it were not for the glint in her eye, her body would have seemed lifeless, limp and beaten.

"Tell Dad from me, this bloody hurts," she sighed heavily and gently squeezed his hand.

◆

THE PHONE rang out through the house. For a moment, she mistook it as part of her dream, but it didn't stop.

"Vivien! The phone! I'm sleeping."

Joanna craned her neck around the door. The landing light was still on but there was no sound.

"Vivien!"

The ringing stopped but the phone hadn't been picked up. It didn't concern her though; she relaxed back into her sleeping position hoping to nod off after the unwelcome interruption.

Joanna sat bolt upright. The banging was deliberate and persistent. She threw her robe around her shoulders and headed downstairs.

"I'm coming!" she yelled as she approached the door, half expecting her daughter to regale her with the events of another church visit. She was already certain that a second visit to Doctor Cross was on the cards.

"Joanna, thank goodness you're home, there's been an accident."

"Where's Vivien?"

"There was a car accident, Viv was involved. She's at the hospital now."

"Is she alive?"

"Of course she is," Carmen exhaled. "We'll head to the hospital as soon as you're ready."

"Viv has been in an accident?"

"You get ready now."

"Yes, I'll get myself ready. Carmen if you would drive I would be most grateful."

"I arranged for a taxi. It's waiting outside."

Thoughts of the past few months seemed to swell inside Joanna's head. All the fights, the anger and the slamming of doors had seemed so natural and so manageable.

"Joanna everything will be fine. She's strong."

"Don't leave me at the hospital. I couldn't bear waiting in those corridors, if she had to go in for an operation or God forbid…"

"Joanna! She will be alright," Carmen assured. "I won't leave you. I will be there and so will Rena."

"Where is Rena?"

"She went straight to the hospital as soon as we heard."

Joanna bit hard on her index finger and watched the pink fluffy dice rock back and forth as the taxi turned a corner.

"Why wasn't I informed first?" Joanna demanded. "I'm her mother. Why wasn't I informed?"

"I was contacted by David, Viv's date, he rang me. He's a friend of mine. He only contacted me first because he knew my number. Please, don't be offended."

Joanna stared straight ahead as the driver swung into the accident and emergency unit.

"I'll get this. You go inside."

The words fell on deaf ears. It was lucky that Carmen was paying; as Joanna darted through the sliding doors before the taxi had come to a halt.

"My daughter, Vivien Goddard. Where can I find her?"

The lady looked up calmly from her desk; her magnifying lenses were distracting. Behind, a nurse leant forward, and looked as though she would be more of assistance.

"If you'll come with me Mrs Goddard."

"What's happened to my daughter?"

"Your daughter has minors injuries, considering what happened, she has bruising on her back and shoulders. We're going to do a scan as a precaution."

Joanna faltered as the nurse turned towards her.

"Try to stay calm Mrs Goddard."

They continued down a long ward.

"She's at the very end. Her friend David is sat beside her."

The nurse turned to leave but was stopped in her tracks by a forceful hand.

"She needs medical assistance."

"Miss Goddard has been seen to. We'll check on her in a short while."

Joanna hurried to her daughter's side and put a trembling hand through her hair.

"Oh my baby. Sweetie are you alright?"

"Sore."

Joanna looked on in dismay. How could her daughter have ended up in this hospital bed? Her face, white and drawn, her hands bandaged, face expressionless and her voice even more so.

"Baby don't talk. You know it's Mummy though, don't you?"

"I won't talk, if you promise never to say the word Mummy again."

Viv was in hospital but she wasn't stupid.

"You sleep baby."

Joanna straightened and adjusted herself in her seat, happy just to sit beside her daughter until it was time to go home.

"Mrs Goddard? My name is David…"

"You need no introduction. You're the reason my baby is lying in a hospital bed."

"It wasn't David's fault. It was an accident," Viv quietly groaned.

"Mrs Goddard, I had no right taking your daughter out. It was purely selfish, and if I hadn't convinced her that taking a ride on my bike was such a good idea, we wouldn't be in this hospital."

"I don't need an explanation. I need you to go."

He did so, not wanting to inflict any more pain than he

already had. Carmen met a solemn looking David as she entered the ward.

"How is she doing?"

"Amazing. She even has a sense of humour considering what's happened."

"What did Joanna say?"

That needed no explanation. David couldn't even meet Carmen's gaze.

"It's not your fault," she sighed. "Why don't we go and have a drink? Could you tell me what happened?"

"I explained everything to the police, they took a statement, no-one else was seriously injured..."

"David, what happened to Viv? You told me over the phone the car never stopped; it only swerved after Viv was knocked out of the way. She could have been killed."

David knew the answer could be saved for another day. Moments later, Rena made her entrance.

"Where did you get to young lady?"

"I needed some fresh air."

"Mr Lancer?" The nurse came over, clutching the obligatory chart. "I've spoken with Mrs Goddard, naturally she'll be staying with her daughter tonight. She suggests you might want to go home and get some rest."

David had no doubt that the affable nurse was sincere, he was however dubious about Mrs Goddard's sentiments.

"David, it might be for the best," Carmen suggested.

"Come back tomorrow morning. Don't look so concerned, the patient will be well looked after," the nurse added.

David ran his hands through his hair, deliberating.

"You're right, if you need me you can reach me on my mobile, Carmen."

David soon found himself in the hospital foyer alone, not sure where to go, or what to do next. Home seemed a futile option. Was he to crack open a beer and then go to sleep as if nothing had happened? Should he wander the streets? There was one place where he felt he could find some sanctuary. He headed towards Elm Drive.

*"Come home Dad. Come home. Leave America now!"*
The words echoed in her head like a bad dream, she was awake, but every muscle in her body was stiff, she felt trapped inside a useless vessel. 'Stupid dreams', she thought to herself, it was the same stupid dream she had had for over a year. The dream where she foresaw her father's fatal accident. They were beginning to become a burden.

"Baby, how are you feeling? My brave Vivien," her mother lingered, stroking her arm gently as if she was a china doll.

"Mum, can we go home?"

Joanna didn't hesitate; she summoned a nurse faster than Viv had time to draw breath.

"How are you feeling this morning Vivien?" the nurse said.

Viv could not describe how she felt, because she couldn't accurately remember what had happened.

"There was an accident, wasn't there? I can't really remember."

"That's right Vivien. An ambulance was called and you were brought in last night. Your friend David was with you."

"David," she whispered quietly to herself. She could feel the missing pieces of the puzzle coming back together.

"Do you remember what happened?"

"Can I go home now?"

Viv sunk back in her pillows; the pain was exhausting but bearable. She closed her eyes and hoped she would be carried out of the hospital as unaware as when she had been brought in.

The church door opened abruptly, creaking loudly on its rusty hinges. The six chairs he had pushed together hadn't been the most appropriate sleeping arrangement, but it was by far the best.

"Gregory! You frightened me to death," David panted, trying to compose himself from his uncomfortable sleep.

"Sorry, I thought I'd come and see how you're doing. You could have slept on the couch you know."

Gregory Hines was pleased to see his friend. The occasional homeless person asked for refuge but not many Mediums asked to stop a night in church. The irony of the situation was not lost on the Church President.

"Thanks for letting me stay here. I just couldn't face going home last night. I needed to collect my thoughts and I'm always at peace when I'm here, not that I actually slept."

"I couldn't sleep much either, after you told me about

the accident. I was up most of the night praying."

"I appreciate that."

"Are you off to the hospital this morning?"

"Right now actually, I'm still a bit shaken by the whole episode."

"She's safe David. Perhaps you need to talk to her about what actually happened."

"Do you mean how she survived?"

"You're her friend, you'll know what to say."

Joanna was fussing. It was deliberate and mostly for show. Rena and Carmen had been invited round for mid-morning tea and biscuits.

"Help yourselves to biscuits. You know I have herbal if that's not to your liking Carmen?"

"Joanna, everything is perfect. I think Viv would like a biscuit though," she remarked; peering over her hostess's shoulder to the disgruntled 'patient' on the sofa.

"Sweetheart, you look uncomfortable."

"I am."

"Would you like a chocolate biscuit?"

"I want the use of my legs back. I think I have too many pillows propping me up. Mum how many have you put back there? I'm about a mile away from the sofa."

"I think we have our Viv back," Rena chuckled as she started on her fifth chocolate biscuit.

On returning home, Joanna had insisted on buying flowers for her daughter's convalescence. To Viv, it felt like a wake. The strong scent of lilies unnerved her; it was a familiar smell.

After thirty minutes of fussing Joanna came to a stand-still. They were faced with a silence stronger than the pungent smell of lilies.

"Joanna, thank you for the tea. I'm sure you want to spend time with Viv. If you need anything don't hesitate to call, and don't even think of cooking, I'll bring something over later."

This was a big relief to Joanna who hadn't cooked in years, she'd almost forgotten how. The door banged behind them.

"We have lovely neighbours don't we darling?"

"That's not what you were saying the other day."

Joanna ventured forward, and perched precariously on the glass coffee table.

"It's a beautiful morning. Would you like to walk in the close?"

"The doctor said I should rest."

"Of course."

"What happened to David?" Viv asked quietly.

"I told that man to go away. If it wasn't for him…" Joanna angered quickly.

"He did try to help! I heard him yelling, he was trying to warn me."

"The police are coming over later to take a statement. You tell them that man put you in harm's way."

"It was not his fault!"

Joanna stood up, rocking the table as she went into the kitchen to light up. The doorbell rang. For once, Viv relaxed back as her mother would have to get the door today.

"If it's the police they're early," she huffed.

"Mum. The door."

The police were not early.

"I told you to keep away, haven't you caused enough damage?"

"Please could I see Viv? I need to apologise to her and to you."

Had she had a large drink in her hand she probably would have thrown it at him. But his few apologetic words and genuine face stirred something inside her, and without saying a word gave way for his entrance.

"You have a visitor Vivien. Clearly not the police."

Joanna took a long drag of her cigarette and sat at the kitchen table, awaiting the grand apology.

"You have to sit by me, I can't turn."

"I brought you some gooseberry jam from the church sale. Four jars in fact."

"Makes a change from lilies, I guess."

Viv looked at the jam, thankful that he hadn't offered a motorbike magazine.

"I can't begin to say how sorry I am. If I could turn the clock back I would have put myself in your place."

"Don't say that," she interjected. "These things can happen, you never think they can happen to you though. Plus, I'm a bit more insulated than you. I think my flab broke the fall," she giggled.

"I'm waiting for an apology!" Joanna announced, as if she had been in the accident and not Viv.

"Mum, can you leave us in private, please?" The last thing Viv wanted was a scene.

"I'll be upstairs," Joanna replied curtly.

They waited a moment, eyes meeting as soon as they heard the door close above.

"Sorry about the trouble I've caused between you and your mother."

"There's been trouble since I was eight years old. Believe me, it's not you."

"Can you remember what happened?"

"Sort of," Viv leaned forward. "You saw the car, didn't you?"

David sat back and looked at the gooseberry jam, contemplating.

"This is going to taste great. They only shifted twenty at the church sale though."

"What are you talking about?"

"No Viv, I didn't see the car," he replied, placing the jam back in its bag.

"Please tell me the truth about last night. What happened?"

"I want to tell you, but you need to rest, it can wait for another time."

"Tell me."

"I knew a car was coming. I knew it was heading your way and I had to race to get to you. I foresaw it before I heard the engine roar, but I couldn't get to you in time."

"I still don't understand. How did you know it was coming? Are you saying you didn't see the car?"

"I had a premonition, as I stood in the middle of that road, I knew something was about to happen."

David was convinced that Viv didn't understand; it was

sometimes hard for him to understand.

"Have you ever been to a place and for some reason it doesn't feel right? The atmosphere, the way it smells, something is telling you that the place isn't where you belong, and you feel scared for absolutely no reason at all? I felt like that only moments before the car appeared, only I can visualise it too."

"I think I know what you mean. Something similar happened to me once."

"Tell me about it."

"I was on a train going to see my aunt and cousins. It was 8am and there was a rowdy gang of boys on the train. I think they were travelling to a football match. For some reason I felt scared, which is weird because there was a nice family sitting near me," Viv paused. "But I felt more scared than when my Mum got drunk. Moments before the train pulled away, I jumped off and didn't go. I still don't know why I did it."

David leaned closer to Viv, and slowly said, "I think we understand each other."

"But that was years ago. I was sixteen, only a silly kid."

Viv unwittingly let David hold her, for a moment she felt embarrassed, like a teenager suddenly realising her crush was real.

"How are the other people doing?" she asked, as she gently pulled back not wanting to seem that she was enjoying the moment.

"No-one else was injured. The guy who was driving was very shaken up though."

"I could have died, they could have died. They swerved

out of the way to avoid me, I remember that."

David didn't want to seem to be contradictory. After all, Viv had experienced one of the most terrifying moments a human being can go through, but he knew it wasn't the truth. David watched her face put the pieces in place, in that order. It helped her control the situation.

"I'll leave the jam on the kitchen table. I'll go upstairs and apologise to your mother."

"You don't have to apologise for anything. She's blaming you because you're here. If my Dad were alive…"

"I'll go up anyway," he interrupted.

Viv put her head back on the pillow and watched his slender figure tiptoe upstairs.

The carpet cushioned the sound but the even measured steps reminded her of her father's.

David stood in the centre of the landing, he had four doors to choose from. He decided that the room straight ahead was as good a choice as any. He knocked lightly and waited for a reply. As he listened, he could hear nothing but the sound of his own heart thumping. He put his hand on the cold brass doorknob and ventured inside; it was the spare room. Boxes were piled on top of each other and an old dusty mattress lay unused. It was an unloved room and the sharp breeze from the half-opened window made him shudder.

"What are you doing in here?"

"Mrs Goddard, I was just coming to apologise."

"You thought you'd find me tucked up in that box, did

you?" she remarked sarcastically. "If you don't mind..."
she gestured a firm but cold hand in the direction of the
landing.

"I came to apologise."

"Would you leave, please. I've had enough bad omens
in this house to last a lifetime."

"What does that mean?"

"My husband, it means my husband. He caused this rift
between my daughter and me, and now you've come into
our lives and I can see history repeating itself. That
charming swagger of yours, the foreign accent, it makes
you some irresistible creature to my daughter. You don't
fool me, you must be ten years older than her anyway!"

"I'm twenty-nine years old."

"Just keep away."

He had outstayed his welcome but despite Joanna's
outburst, he couldn't promise that he wouldn't return.

## Three Weeks Later...

THE CENTRAL library was the last place that David Lancer
usually found himself on a Saturday afternoon. He had
seen Viv briefly over the past three weeks, but was fiercely
kept at bay by a mother continuing on her neurotic
downward path. The last time David had spoken to Viv,
he learned that Joanna had booked herself for regular
appointments with Doctor Cross.

"Can I help you young man?"

"That would be great, I'm useless with computers. I was
hoping to find old newspaper stories on the Internet."

"Well, I think it would be best if you took a look at the microfiche. If you'd follow me, I'll help you get it started."

"Can I have you're name ma'am?"

"Gladys. You're American aren't you?" she said, sounding extremely pleased with herself.

David smiled, she reminded him of his grandmother. He extended his hand, Gladys looking coy, extended hers.

"My name is David. I'm looking for articles appearing on Sunday 17th July 1998."

"Follow me," she said, giving him a playful wink.

Once David was seated, he knew that he would have some explaining to do later on. He had phoned Viv moments before he entered the library.

*"Can you remember what date it was when you went to see your aunt and cousins?"*

*"Do you mean the time when I hopped off the train?"*

*"Yes, can you remember the date?"*

*"I saved the train ticket. Why?"*

*"I'll explain later. Could you get the ticket now?"*

Gladys carefully explained the instructions; every word precise and deliberate, enjoying the company of this polite young man.

"And if you need any more help, please don't hesitate to call me. I'll be sitting at my desk, which is just over there. Alright dear?"

He watched Gladys from his peripheral vision waddling back to her desk. He felt relaxed enough to scan the information in his own time. The stories were varied and similar to any of the present headlines. *'One of the hottest days on record – Hunt for killer of three...'* the list went on. He was looking for something much more specific.

He shuffled his chair closer to the screen, and at face value, nothing seemed to leap off the page.

'What's this then?' he wondered to himself, enlarging a small column which had caught his attention.

> *'Shooting on train. Several passengers injured as gunman fired at random. Three men were wounded, though no-one was seriously injured.'*

◆

"I HATE good-byes. You will come to see me won't you?" Rena felt tearful at the prospect of her new surroundings.

"You're going to Warwick not Warsaw!"

Viv felt closer to her friend than she had done all summer and now she was leaving.

"I feel bad we haven't made the most of our time recently. Too wrapped up in my petty messes."

"I wouldn't call recovering from a road accident petty."

Viv shrugged.

"By the way, what do you think of David, Rena?"

"Nice. He likes you doesn't he?"

"He probably feels obliged, especially after the accident."

"Don't be stupid. Men don't spend their time around

girls they don't like. Help me with this suitcase would you?"

"I only ask, because the night of the accident I remember you gave me this look. I was worried that I'd stepped on your territory. Had I?"

Rena lugged the suitcase in the boot, rocking the car in the process.

"I did like him, but I didn't fancy... maybe I did a little because he's attractive but definitely not my type."

"I'm sorry if I hurt you."

"You didn't, besides I'm off to university and if I can't find a gorgeous man there, then where can I find one?" Rena smiled, shutting the boot and sidling up to her friend.

"Viv, I want you to promise me something. Focus on your life now. You've done all you can to help with your Mum."

"I will."

"All set darling?" Carmen asked airily.

"Ready when you are."

Carmen made her way over to the girls.

"Ravishing in pink, Carmen!" Viv called out, quite out of character.

"Thank you dear, at least someone noticed," she sighed prodding her daughter in the arm. "Remember," she whispered. "Just because Rena's at university doesn't mean you have to stop coming around. You're welcome anytime."

"Thanks Carmen and vice versa," she hesitated.

"Final hugs. I hate final hugs," Rena moaned.

Viv was quick to pull away before any premature tears began to tumble.

"Rena wait, I need to ask you something."

"Top secret?" Rena mocked.

"I just wanted to ask you about this whole Spiritualism thing which David seems so intent on. I have my own thoughts but what do you think it's all about?"

"You want me to explain it now?" Rena felt exasperated with Viv's timing.

"In a nutshell," Viv naively ventured.

"It's just a part of life most people can't accept or don't want to understand."

"Something about ghosts?"

"Spirits. Trust me I was the biggest sceptic but when you see it for yourself, you'll know it's real. Just ask David."

"The only reason I ask you is because everything he does or says sounds cryptic. Like he's building up to something."

"Maybe he is. David has his strange little ways, my Mum has filled me in on him."

As Carmen and Rena reversed out of the driveway and into Winter Road, Viv gave thought to when she would actually see her friend again. It hadn't crossed her mind up until this point but would they actually keep in touch? How much of what they said was for show and what was for real? The car was now out of sight and a familiar sound disturbed the peace of the quiet little close.

"I thought I told him to stay away?" Joanna didn't wait around to tell him so in person.

"I missed Rena didn't I?" David caught his breath.

"Yes, I'm glad you did. I had her all to myself."

"You'll see her soon Viv."

"Sure."

"Could I come inside?"

"I don't think so, you're not exactly on my Mum's favourite list. I think you're probably on my Mum's most wanted list. Do you fancy going for a drive? You can come in my car unless you're one of those guys who can't stand being driven by a woman, are you?"

"No ma'am," he smiled, a smile which looked like a polite cover up for, 'Yes I am'.

As Viv pulled out of the driveway she asked him where he wanted to go.

"You've never been to my home. Would you like to go there?"

"Sure. I'd like to see where you live. I also have something to ask you."

"That sounds ominous."

"It's about the accident. I haven't been completely honest with you and I think you know that."

The car quietly whirred out of the cul-de-sac as if she was tiptoeing away like a naughty child, hoping her mother wouldn't find out.

"What would you like to ask me?"

"I'd like to be sitting down, not moving at least."

"You'll get to meet my partner in crime. Probably the best guy I know."

Viv felt relieved, she was finally being allowed a peek in David's forbidden world. Up until now he'd never mentioned anything about his life or where he lived.

"Joe's Garage? I thought you said you part owned it."

"I do. Joe's my partner."

"Shouldn't you have equal billing?"

The sign was unmistakable in large blue font in front of what looked like a genuine garage.

"The bastard hogged the whole sign. He said it was an accident and that he got carried away. Something about his artistic side coming alive," David laughed as he faked mock anger.

David made his way over old rusty cans and tyres that littered the driveway. Had it not been for their reliability as mechanics, this place would have looked like a business about to go bankrupt. Viv followed in trepidation, wondering whether any killer dogs lay lurking under the scrap.

"Don't look so scared."

"Me scared? You're talking to the girl who endured two weeks on the sofa listening to eight hours of my Mum each day. I'm not scared of anything."

"Oh yeah?"

"Yeah," she replied in louder tones.

"You back then?" a gruff voice called out from the kitchen. Viv stepped past David and into the hallway. It was dark, with light desperately trying to filter through the orange Sixties-style curtains which probably hadn't seen a wash since that era.

"Come through Viv."

A largish man, with a shock of red hair stood chewing a bacon sandwich.

"Hey Joe, do we get a "hello" or will we have to talk to

the back of your head?"

"Guest?" he turned surprised. "'Scuse me, I think my vision is blurred. This is a woman right?"

Viv smiled politely, though rooted to the spot. The imposing six-foot figure lurched towards her like a bear.

"This is a very rare and welcome occurrence. My name is Joe," he garbled, one word seeming to merge with the other. "Just stay there and I'll make you the best bacon sandwich you'll ever eat. I'm a great cook."

Viv had yet to muster the courage to speak and was still giggling, she was actually enjoying this unusual introduction. His strangeness was disarming and she realised why David wasn't bothered about him stealing the limelight, so to speak.

"He's not a great cook. I live with him," David added, as he opened the fridge door to a horrifying sight. "What the hell is that?"

"My socks. You know how hot my feet get running this shop. Thought I'd cool them down."

"Sure. Cold socks are the best," Viv nodded.

"Viv, I'd offer you a beer but I fear it's been contaminated."

"I'll take my chances."

"Hey, I like this girl. Are you gonna introduce me?"

"I thought you did that yourself?"

David handed over a beer.

"My name is Joe, and you are?"

"Viv."

"Can I call you Vivien? I think Vivien is a beautiful name for a lady."

"Yes you can," she said gladly. This compliment pleased her immensely. Her Dad called her Vivien, her mother insisted on it and she saw no reason why someone else shouldn't. Secretly she preferred Vivien.

"I hate to break up this beautiful introduction but…"

"Well, well, well, our Romeo here is jealous of our mutual affection. You can't stop it you know, if we're destined to be together you can't stop true love."

Viv was highly entertained at this friendly game of tug-of-war. David, who she imagined would be amiable in all circumstances looked rather put out, opened his beer can and took a large swig.

"Come on David, I'm only playing."

"Someone ought to be looking after the shop. We could have a line of customers waiting."

"But my socks aren't done."

Viv went to laugh, but spat out a mouthful of beer instead.

"This is the girl for me. Even has the same habits," Joe moved in closer and playfully hugged his dribbling guest.

"I'm going out front," David said abruptly.

Suddenly the playful introduction came to an uneasy end. Joe didn't know where to put his face and made his way over to the fridge.

"Cool enough?" Viv offered. She had to say something, she suddenly felt bad for Joe who was only trying to make her feel at ease.

"Er, yeah, they are actually."

"Did I do something wrong?"

"No love, not at all. It's me. Don't know when to keep

my big mouth shut. He must like you a lot. I hope I didn't offend?"

"No way," Viv replied a little surprised. A man who could make her laugh and feel comfortable, is a man sent directly from the gods.

"Nice to meet you Vivien. I'll go and see if the boy is okay. You stay here and finish your beer. Can finish my sandwich if you like?"

She declined politely and pushed the plate out of arm's reach. David reappeared.

"Where did you go?"

"Out front to see if there were any customers."

Viv was hanging on his words in the hope that he would manage some semblance of an explanation, but to no avail.

"I'd show you the rest of the house but I fear this is the most presentable."

He pulled up a chair close to Viv.

"It's a guy thing, what happened a moment ago."

"Joe made me feel comfortable."

David clearly wasn't, and hovered over to a corkboard covered with postcards. It was a distraction at least.

"I love postcards. Are those from your friends?"

"More like happy customers. This one is my favourite."

"Big Sur, California. What a great name."

"Have you been to California, Viv?"

"Only in my dreams and in movies. Why did you come over to England anyway?"

"I needed a change of scenery, plus I have family over here, which spurred me on to make the change."

"My Dad loved America, quite fitting really."

"What do you mean?"

"This may sound weird but I'm glad he passed away somewhere he loved than say, at home where he was unhappy."

"It doesn't sound weird at all."

"You know what, I've just realised I know nothing about your life or your family."

"Well, I'll tell you sometime."

"How about now?"

"I'd rather talk about you, tell me what you wanted to say earlier."

Viv took one last gulp, she hadn't finished the drink, in fact it dawned on her that it was quite revolting.

"It's about the accident. I need to know, did you save me?"

"I couldn't have Viv. I was at least ten metres away."

"But I was pushed to the side of the road. I felt it."

"You were, but not by me. Your Guardian Angel intervened to make sure you were safe."

"Angel?"

"As I approached I knew I was too late, and so I asked your Guardian Angel to intervene. A barrier was put between you and the car. The car hit the barrier and you were thrown onto the bank."

"That couldn't have happened. That's ridiculous."

"It happened Viv. Your Guardian Angel is with you all the time. You only have to ask for help."

"It's crazy though. Maybe I had a magical, invisible hero who pushed me out of harm's way that night.

Oh my God."

The sound of the kitchen chair screeched as Viv rose to her feet.

"I remember a fantastic, silly story my Dad told me before I went to sleep."

Viv was unaware that Joe had breezed back into the kitchen with a very large tyre.

"Viv, just relax and tell me."

"My Dad once told me a story about people he called silent heroes. They watch out for us, making sure we're okay. I was so upset that John Wayne wasn't mine. He said that these heroes are capable of extraordinary acts of kindness and foresight and are sometimes able to help out in circumstances which are otherwise out of our control."

Joe sensing the moment wasn't appropriate, decided not to mention that a grateful customer had offered them a wheel, from a genuine Formula One racing car, and made his way out of the back door.

"Go on."

"My Dad confided in me about an incident which occurred one night before I was born. My parents were coming back from a weekend away, it was 3am and they were both exhausted. Mum was driving and my Dad was fidgeting with the radio, and hadn't noticed that Mum was falling in and out of sleep. Her arms became limp and she let go of the wheel. The car swerved over to the fast lane towards the central barrier. Dad looked up to see my Mum's head flopped down and the car about to impact. The steering wheel turned and the car pulled back into the middle lane. Dad never even touched the steering wheel."

"Have you made the connection between your parents' near miss and yours?"

"Maybe."

"Could you entertain the idea that your Dad intervened at that moment?"

Viv took a step back, evaluating all that was implicated.

"Maybe. I don't know. I feel really strange just thinking about it."

Viv grabbed at her neck, feeling the same sensation as she did when she first heard the news from America.

"Relax Viv. You need water."

Water was the last thing on her mind; she wanted to find out what really happened to her father.

◆

THE SMELL, which greeted Viv on her return home later that afternoon, was nothing short of foul. Not in all this time had it ever been this bad.

"Mum, have you been sick?"

"I'm not well, Vivien."

"You were sick on the carpet. Why haven't you cleaned up? This place is foul. Bottles, glasses, wine…"

"Because you weren't here to help me."

"This is not my job. I'm not your carer."

"I'm your only mother. You should have been here."

Viv found it in her heart to forgive her mother's outburst.

"I'll clean this up."

"No, I'm doing it."

"You're in a state Mum, I'll do it."

"Are you ashamed of me? Would you rather go off with your freaky boyfriend?"

"What has he done that was so bad? The accident wasn't his fault. He has apologised and apologised. He can't even come over without fear of being verbally abused."

"I just don't want you seeing that church freak."

"He's not a freak! Why are you so scared of the church? What happened?"

"What does that mean?"

"Dad was into Spiritualism wasn't he? I bet he went to that very church I went to."

"I don't want you going to that church again."

"Why? For once just tell me the reason."

Luckily a chair broke her mother's slump as she wiped her chin with a dirty sleeve.

"Your father."

"What about him?"

"He went there, to that church you go on about."

"What's wrong with going to church?"

"He came back with all these crazy ideas and beliefs. Idiotic ideas that when people die they don't actually die. Their Spirit lives on!" she dramatised, her hand flailing in distress. "Do you know that he said I have guides, angels, people who protect and look after me. Well, what a bloody great job they have done so far, eh?"

"Mum, please calm down."

"He ruined our relationship with his beliefs. He wanted to tell you everything, all he had learnt with his stupid books, but I never let him."

"Dad never ruined anything."

"Oh, he did my darling. Did you know why your precious father was in America? Do you want to know why?"

"He was on a business trip of course."

"Business trip? He was almost broke."

"Dad had a job."

"Daddy was fired days before he left for America."

"What?"

"The point was he left for America. A supposed job offer he had to investigate. What a load of bullshit!" She took another swig this time and swallowed every drop. A flash of sadness appeared and faded just as quickly.

"I don't know what to say. I thought Dad was on a business trip. He would've told me."

"Your precious Dad wasn't all he seemed. Now, I've told you, will you promise not to go to that church again?"

"You didn't tell me anything. You're drunk, of course you're going to say everything that was bad about my Dad."

"I don't want you going. I can't keep having this fight with you Vivien."

"I can't either. I'm worn out."

"You go to that church again and I'm not having you back here to tonight."

"Then I guess you're on your own."

The congregation seemed to have grown in size. The church was packed thirty minutes before the service was due to start.

"We're all very eager here."

Viv looked to see a very petite elderly lady, standing next to her or rather being squashed against her.

"It certainly looks that way. I thought I was early."

"No dear, the service starts anytime now."

Viv stood on tiptoes. David seemed to appear out of nowhere, and stood imposingly on the platform.

"Oh this young man is superb. I'm so glad he's on tonight."

"His name is David isn't it?" she ventured knowingly. Maybe she would be able to wheedle some information out of this very amiable lady.

"Yes and he's very good. He has been at this church for quite a while now. His readings are always accurate."

"Have you ever had a reading?"

"I have. He gave me a very specific date on which something significant was going to happen on March 28th of this year. It turned out to be the date my daughter announced she was pregnant with my first grandchild."

"Surely it was a coincidence."

"Maybe, but it didn't half bring a smile to my face. My name is Rosemary Matthews by the way, I'm a church regular. And you are?" she smiled offering her hand.

"Viv Goddard."

"Oh my. Are you by any chance Simon Goddard's daughter?"

"Yes, that's right – did you know my Dad?"

"I am so sorry my dear. I knew your father from church, I spoke to him occasionally."

"Thank you. He came here often didn't he?"

"Yes he did. He was such an amiable man. He spent most of his time with David as a matter of fact, always in deep discussions before and after the service."

"Really?"

The information was disconcerting. The fact that David had failed to mention the closeness of their relationship added to her growing suspicions. Instead of waiting to be enthralled like the rest of the congregation, she left, leaving behind a puzzled Mrs Matthews.


Carmen was extremely accommodating considering she had just put on a face-mask and shared an uncanny resemblance to Hannibal Lecter.

"You have perfect timing Viv. In fact, you'll be able to help me wash this off. I fear we might need scourers," she tutted to herself.

"I was supposed to be at a service tonight. David asked me specially."

Viv was finding it hard to adjust herself in the chaise longue, and remain serious at the same time.

"Viv come and join me on the sofa," Carmen offered, watching Viv's clumsy attempts to get comfortable. "I may look like a monster but I don't bite."

Feeling a great deal more at ease, and with the fire slowly burning behind, she plonked herself beside Carmen.

"I just found out that David and my Dad were close. He

never even mentioned it to me. He's like a walking puzzle."

"There's probably a reason for it. Maybe you give out signals that you don't wish to converse about your father."

"But we do, most of the time, somehow he always crops into conversation. How could he not tell me?"

"Come with me. I would like to show you something."

She followed Carmen into her dining room. It was polished to within an inch of its life. Viv could tell she hadn't cooked in a while.

"Do you like this picture?"

Viv had passed by this particular picture many times. A beautiful painting of the most perfect sea view imaginable.

"Yes, it's beautiful. Is it from memory, or of an actual place?"

"Both."

"Where is it?"

"California."

"Oh."

"Your father loved this painting. He wanted to know where he could get another. I said it was an exclusive painting by one of my favourite pupils. He was determined to have a painting just like it, and I told him how to find the artist. I'm afraid it was I who made their first introduction. I told your father that David was our local mechanic and had an interest in Spiritualism."

"Why did my Dad like this painting so much?"

"I told him it was a place I had been to before. A beautiful view in California that could only be experienced in the flesh. Your father loved America."

"Can I ask you a question? Please be honest with me."

"I'll do my best."

"Did you know anything about my Dad being fired? My Mum told me he was fired days before he left for America and that is part of the reason he went – a job opportunity."

"I knew, he told me. He felt it would be a good opportunity to get some space from your mother and their problems, and he had a possible job opportunity out there."

"What was it?"

The conversation halted as Carmen's bell sounded several times. Viv remained in the dining room and gazed at the painting. She closed her eyes and imagined how that sea would smell, the flowers, the sand. At that moment David walked into the room.

"You never came to the service? I was worried."

"I'm sorry, I did come but I left. I wasn't in the mood. I had an almighty row with Mum. I did however meet a lady called Rosemary. You never told me that you and my Dad were close?"

"I wouldn't say we were close. We just shared a common interest, I liked his company."

"So, did my Dad tell you to contact me or was it a coincidence?"

"I'd call it fate but he did tell me we should meet up, that was before he left for America."

"So, are you only hanging around with me as a loyalty to him?"

"Of course not. I enjoy your company. I also know what you must be going through. My parents died three years ago, tomorrow."

Viv looked to Carmen for an answer, she couldn't find the words herself.

"Viv, I didn't come round to make you feel sad."

"David I am so sorry," Viv felt embarrassed at her selfishness. In all this time she'd never considered that her friends might have troubles of their own.

"Thank you, but please don't feel sad."

"You should have told me."

"Listen, I have something in my pocket that might cheer you up," David's innocent comment registered. Viv glanced over at Carmen for a second time, but for an entirely different reason. They had to suppress their giggles.

"You ladies, are very rude," he grinned. David slid two tickets onto the dining table. Viv moved closer to inspect. "You said once that your instinct told you to get off that train, remember?"

"Yes." she said a little surprised.

"You were right to."

David reached inside his leather coat and produced a newspaper cutting.

"This is what I found in the library. Did you get that train ticket that I asked you for?"

Luckily she had never thrown it away, and reached inside her coat pocket to find the withered old ticket

David had requested.

"There was a shooting on that train just as it pulled into Manchester station."

"You are joking?"

"No-one was seriously injured. I dug a little deeper, and found out that it happened on coach number four; your coach."

David exhaled deeply and gave Viv the article.

"That is impossible."

"I spoke to the local reporter assigned to that case. He's still at the paper after all these years. A bullet pierced seat G12, your seat."

Viv had seen enough, and pushed it aside; it was becoming too real, the evidence, the stories, and the coincidences.

"Where is this going? If your job is to freak me out, mission accomplished. What with the accident as well."

"These are plane tickets. I booked them three months ago. I fly out to California tomorrow morning and I want you to come with me."

Viv brushed the comment aside and allowed herself a nervous giggle.

"What's so funny?"

"You are David. You are funny. California?"

"I go every year. I go and pay my respects. I might be out of order saying this, but I thought you might be able to put some closure on what happened to your Dad. I know you have some unanswered questions about why he was there."

"But you said you booked the tickets three months ago,

you never even knew me then."

"If I'm honest this second ticket was never intended for you. Joe usually comes with me, but I asked him if he would give up his ticket for you."

"How long do you go for?"

"As long as I need to."

"It sounds like an opportunity too good to miss," Carmen interjected.

"I can't go. I'm not prepared. My Mum…"

"Insignificant details Viv. I will watch your mother and you need a holiday."

"Here's the ticket, you know where the airport is. Terminal 3 at 7am. I want you there."

"Where are you going?" Viv panicked, suddenly feeling an enormous amount of pressure.

"To pack," he grinned. "Carmen, I'll send you a postcard."

"I'd like that."

Viv stood deliberating the pros and cons, "What should I do?"

She left the cosy confines of Carmen's home contemplating the prospect of leaving home for the very first time.

The suitcase was dusty and had lay unused since she was fifteen, when the family had taken their last holiday together. She searched through her clothes and decided that she didn't really know what the weather in California would be like. She chucked everything in that she could think of, and zipped up the case. It was now

6.00am as she peered through the curtains impatiently awaiting her taxi. The house stood very still now, her mother had long since gone to bed. As she paced around the living room, the smell of the carpet made her feel uneasy, it reminded her of the fragile state her mother was still in.

"Vivien, I knew you would come home. I knew," she smiled. Joanna stood at the foot of the stairs, ghost-like. "What's this suitcase doing by the stairs?"

"Mum I'm going away for a while. I need a break from all this. I'm going with David."

"What are you talking about?" she blurted as she threw back the curtains, conscious of the car turning into the driveway.

"I'll be gone no more than two weeks."

"Where are you going?"

"California."

"You're crazy. Off to California with a stranger? Over my dead body."

"I'll ring you when I get there."

Viv, stronger than her Mum, pushed past and felt her weaken.

"I love you Mum but you can't tell me not to go."

"If you love me, you'll stay."

"Don't blackmail me Mum, just be happy for me, please!"

Viv stepped out into the chilly morning, a renewed and hopeful light came through the misty clouds as the taxi driver stepped forward to assist.

"Hey Vivien, nice to see you again."

Viv looked closely at the man, he didn't register with her.

"I'm sorry have we met before?"

"You fell asleep on my back seat. You can't remember eh? You girls and your drink," he muttered lightly as he lifted the case into the boot.

"Baby this is ridiculous, whatever I said I didn't mean it," she pleaded grabbing onto Viv's arms in desperation.

"I know you don't mean it Mum. I want you to get help. I want you to see Doctor Cross again, but I can't do it for you. There have to be changes when I come back."

"If I get better you'll come back?"

"I'll come back anyway. I need this holiday Mum and you need to get better. I think we're starting to suffocate each other. Time apart is a good thing and this is an opportunity for me."

"I've finally done it haven't I? I've pushed you away, I've driven you into the arms of that lunatic. I felt this was coming."

Viv ignored this and went in for a hug.

"Just take care of yourself Mum. Don't be scared."

Viv jumped into the back seat. The car pulled away, and Viv watched her mother stand so lonely at the top of the driveway, she was still standing there as they turned the corner.

"Will your Mum be okay?"

"I really hope so. Nice to see you again, though I can't remember you."

"I have one of those faces, Vivien. You know that's a beautiful name for a woman."

◆

Viv had arrived precisely when requested. The check-in desks weren't open, however, and staff were scarce.

"Excuse me miss, could you tell me what time the check-in desk opens?"

"We open at seven. There's a coffee shop over there. You will be able to see when the desk opens."

As Viv turned around to find the shop, the woman seemed to vanish into thin air. No check-in and no David, she was beginning to wonder if it was some half-baked plan that wouldn't actually be taking off.

"You're early."

Viv hadn't heard the footsteps behind but the voice was instantly recognisable.

"David, I was beginning to wonder whether this was a real trip."

"For a girl, I think you've done amazingly well. Just one case!"

David was doing well himself with one large rucksack. He leant in and initiated the embrace.

"Thank you for coming."

"Oh," Viv trembled, reciprocating his affection and enjoying it too. "My Mum wasn't too pleased. I think she's starting to realise I won't be there all the time."

"Good. I've got you all to myself. I was worried you were going to bring her along."

"By the way, the check-in desk opens at seven."

"Viv, I'm a very bad man. Our plane departs midday, I

just wanted to give you plenty of time to get here."

Viv was touched, even though they had several hours to wait.

Departures was just how her father had described.

*"Vivien, you'll never guess where I am?"*

*"Are you calling from the plane?"*

*"No, I'm in Departures and it has some wonderful shops. I've brought you a bottle of your favourite perfume."*

*"Can I come and pick it up?"*

*"Sweetpea, Departures is only for people on flights."*

*"When can I come with you Dad?"*

Departures always excited her father, a gateway to a brand new destination that held endless possibilities. Her quiet thoughts returned to the excitable and nervous energy which filled the expansive hall. Luckily they found two spare seats.

"My Dad loved Departures."

"You're glowing, I've never seen you like this before. Weird."

"You sound like a surfer dude when you say weird."

"What's a surfer dude?"

They erupted into laughter, Viv didn't care how loud she was and who heard, she was allowing herself a small dose of well-deserved happiness.

"You forget kid that I'm a New Yorker at heart. We don't surf."

"You have to know how, I'm counting on it."

"Why do you want to surf?"

"I don't really. I just want to fry and try and shift

my pasty complexion."

"You have that English rose, peaches and cream complexion, beautiful."

Unable to respond due to a rare case of flattery David interjected, "Want to go shopping?"

"I better not, I'm doing everything on cards to begin with."

"This trip is on me. You don't have to worry about a thing. Speaking of, on me, I need a drink. Would you like a drink, on me?"

"Just water, thanks."

He disappeared instantly into a sea of faces. Viv loved people watching. A fat lady, laden with bags, reeking of an overbearing perfume looked disapprovingly as she tottered past. A beautiful little girl, with a gigantic yellow bow atop her black, bouncy curls, came into view.

"One water."

"Do you see that little girl, David? She keeps waving me over."

"Which little girl are you talking about?"

"That one, with the huge yellow bow," Viv pointed out the obvious.

"I can't see her," said David, flicking his eyes from side to side.

Viv laughed, "You must be blind as a bat."

David felt a cold breeze pass through him. He knew instantly what was happening.

"Keep watching her," he said rapidly. His eye lids closed, head dropped, he sat perfectly still. "She's calling your name."

Viv leapt forward towards the girl, a huge man puffing his cigar blocked her view.

"Excuse me," she pushed past straight into the path of another fat lady. They collided, landing in a heap on the floor. Her big red hat bounced off her enviably blonde curls.

"You clumsy girl!"

"Sorry."

Viv scrambled to her feet, brushing herself off, "You weren't even looking where you were going."

The woman grimaced at Viv as she scuttled off. The faces of concerned onlookers parted. The little girl had disappeared.

"She's gone."

David walked over. This time a serious look fixed his face.

"Are you okay?"

"I'm fine. I wonder where she went to?"

"Don't you realise what has just happened? You've just seen Spirit. I can only feel and hear them, but you can actually see them."

"That little girl is a Spirit?"

"Yes, and she was calling out your name."

"Where is she?" Viv looked in all directions.

"She has left you now but she will be back."

"How do you know for certain?"

"Because she is waiting for you in America. I'll let you into a secret. When you open yourself up to the world of Spirit, all things are possible."

◆ ◆ ◆

Viv's eyes flickered momentarily as the flight attendant bumped past her seat. David had been out for almost an hour. The economy class cabin was quiet apart from the low hum of a young boy's Gameboy, sitting one row in front.

'Why do people walk so loudly?' she thought. Her eyes opened. She turned towards the aisle, though no-one was there. She closed her eyes once more and hoped to drift off into a long sleep. The pitter-patter of footsteps passed her seat once more, this time it had become aggravating. She sat bolt upright. The entire cabin was asleep apart from the little boy who was far too engrossed to be running to and fro.

"Miss," she whispered over to an ever-smiling attendant. "I don't mean to be a pest but someone is walking very loudly down the aisle. I'm just wondering if you could tell them to go a little quieter."

"Ma'am, I'm afraid no-one has walked past your seat in the last fifteen minutes or so. Perhaps you were dreaming," she beamed and returned to her colleague.

"It's the little girl," David turned and yawned, smacking his parched lips together, he had been woken too. "She's just playing. The flight attendant is right, no-one has walked past you in the last fifteen minutes."

"Where is she now?"

"Don't be panicked," he gently rubbed her shoulder. "She understands you want to sleep and won't disturb you any more."

"How do you know this?"

"I asked her to let us sleep. Now she is playing further down the cabin so she won't disturb you."

David turned over in his seat and soon all was quiet again. Viv reclined in her seat half hoping to hear the little footsteps again.

"Psst, lady!"

Viv leaned forward, poked her head around the seat in front, it was the young boy, briefly distracted from his game.

"It's okay, I'll keep her quiet for a while. She likes watching my Gameboy."

"What's your name?" Viv whispered back.

"I'm Connor. I'm flying home to LA with my Dad. I just wanted you to know the little girl is sitting with me. She was bugging me too, running up and down the aisle. I lost on level three because of her." He shook his head solemnly.

"You see a little girl with you?"

"Sure. She's nice, she doesn't mean to bug you."

"I can't believe this."

"Anyway, I've got to get back to my game now…"

"Just one more thing. Do you see Spirits all of the time?"

"Sure. My Mom's with me right now."

Viv suddenly felt a surge of panic. She assumed too quickly that the little boy saw Spirit. He could just as easily see her as a proper little girl. He was so calm about seeing her – and 'Yes!' – he did see his mother! Viv felt relieved that she had not upset Connor. She would be more careful in the future, she promised herself. With her sigh of relief came sleep.

The eleven and a half-hour flight finally came in to land in the perfect climes of Los Angeles International Airport. Viv exchanged brief glances with Connor as they departed through the sliding doors. She stood and watched as he moved away with his father. 'What a special little boy he is,' she thought. He reminded her of David.

"We've arrived!" David smiled. "We need to find the bus to take us to the car rental. Once we have the car, we're on our way."

As Viv followed David through the throng of tourists, she realised what had been missing from her life – a sense of adventure. They collected their Toyota, joined the highway and headed in the direction of Santa Monica beach.

"Where are we staying by the way?" Viv asked.

David remained concentrated as he steadily veered into the fast lane.

"I don't know yet. Where would you like to stay?"

"I assumed you would have booked somewhere?"

"No, I never book. You never know where a trip may take you. For all I know we may end up in San Francisco."

David's lack of preparation was glaring and Viv was beginning to feel oppressed by the stifling heat.

"What if all the hotels are booked? What are we going to do?"

"Relax, we're in LA." It suddenly dawned on David

how much Viv reminded him of his mother, who would have had a schedule for absolutely everything. It brought a smile to his face. Viv kept quiet until she reached a familiar scene. The image had remained so vivid in her mind that the reality was full-blown Technicolor glory. Viv took off her seat belt, which prompted David to pull over. Taking her first breath of Santa Monica air was even more freeing than she had imagined. She had experienced this moment a million times before from her father's descriptions, and on his postcards. Santa Monica beach stretched left and right beyond the bonnet of the car. Palm trees lined the promenade offering fans of shade to cool the beautiful afternoon strollers. It was nearing 4pm and the sun cast a hazy glow that seemed to illuminate every person. Viv felt very privileged and wished silently that her father could share the moment.

"Look at the sea!" she gasped. "How come nobody's swimming?"

"Because that water is freezing."

"Oh," she replied a little glum.

"Come on then, pick one."

"Do you mean a hotel?"

"No a palm tree. It's custom to take one with you to Disneyland. You get a ten per cent discount."

"Okay, Mr Sarcastic, what about that one? It's big and bound to have a room."

"It's also very expensive, and I'm not that rich."

All concerns about accommodation had sweated out of her skin, she felt refreshed and ready to camp out on the beach if need be.

"This will do, cheap and cheerful."

The sunlight disappeared as they drove down the ramp into the underground car park, a far cry from beachside luxury but they had arrived.

"Great view. David come and look at this. You don't get this in Ossilton."

"I missed you," he cried, playfully kissing the TV set. "Now this is television! It has every channel you could think of."

"You can't be serious? You've paid all this money and you want to watch television?"

Viv stepped off the balcony and reluctantly slid next to her companion, a little more than anxious that they should be heading for the beach.

"Viv, I just want to ask you if you're okay about sharing the same room?"

"Of course I am. We do have separate beds after all."

David settled further into his pillow. As the minutes rolled by Viv's afternoon by the sea was looking more like a lost opportunity. She was sure he would be asleep within the hour if she didn't take action.

"Heads or tails!" she blurted.

"What?"

"Heads or tails – heads we sit and watch boring TV or tails we go to the beach."

Viv flicked the coin – tails it was.

"Come on then tourist, let's hit the beach now."

In a matter of minutes they had reached Santa Monica

Pier. The stifling heat had turned into something more manageable, and the stiff breeze almost took her breath away as they walked upon the boardwalk. Her mind flashed back to childhood walks along Blackpool Pier. As they strolled arm in arm it was hard to believe they were actually here. For the moment, she had put the little girl right to the back of her mind.

"I wish I could pretend like this for the whole holiday."

"Well you can, this isn't just a trip with an agenda. We're here to have fun too."

"I'll drink to that, if we ever get past all these kids."

"There's a drink stand over there," David tugged at Viv's arm.

As they queued, it was hard not to be distracted by the big wheel silhouetted perfectly by the hazy orange backdrop.

"Do you like heights, Viv?"

"I don't, but I like looking up at the wheel."

"What would you like to drink?"

"Just a cola."

Viv wondered for a moment what American cola tasted like but quickly realised it was the dumbest thought to enter her mind, instead she gazed up at the people having fun.

"Want to go up?"

"I'd sooner have this drink."

Viv wandered ahead and leaned against the cool metal railings. Santa Monica cola was the best.

"How about the big wheel, then?"

"No way."

"You'll love it. You won't get a better view of LA anywhere else."

Viv's eyes fixated on the height restriction board, barring anyone less than 4'6" tall from going on the ride. This was the only moment in her life when she wanted to walk under Mr Turkey's outstretched wing. As the bar came down, she had no alternative but to act as though she was going to enjoy it.

"Is anyone else getting on? I wouldn't like to think we're the only twosome plunging into the ocean."

"Do you ever relax?" David quipped.

Viv looked ahead hoping she would find someone feeling just as nervous as she was.

"There's a little girl in the car above. Is she on her own?"

"There you go, if a little girl can go it alone then you can too," David was craning his neck to see if there was, in fact, somebody in the carriage above.

"Surely they wouldn't allow a little girl to go on her own? Oh my goodness, we're moving. My legs are dangling, this isn't good for my stomach. Do you see the little girl looking at us? Maybe she wants to get off, we should call down to the controller."

"I don't see anybody."

Viv gripped the handle as if her life depended on it. She felt her stomach lurch as the carriage swung higher.

"I know her. It's the girl from the airport. Little girl!"

Viv leant forward and yelled as loud as she could, their carriage was nearing the top now.

"Viv don't shout, you'll scare her away."

"You told me she is a Spirit?"

"She is, but you'll scare her away. You're coming over as aggressive, all she wants to do is make her presence known."

"I want to get down and talk to her. When is this ride going to end?"

The anticipation was unbearable, the ride was a form of slow torture.

The little legs dangling above transfixed Viv, as the carriage swung to and fro. Her little white socks were pulled up properly and her painted black shoes would not have looked out of place on a china doll. The carriage in front dropped beneath the roof of the platform. Viv and David rocked as they waited to get off.

"Sir, there was a little girl in the carriage ahead, did you see where she went?"

"Miss, the car ahead of you was empty."

"No, she was right in front of us. She had a yellow dress, a big bow in her hair, white socks pulled up to her knees..."

"There was nobody in it. I was standing right here."

Viv felt herself being ushered away; David put his arm over her shoulder.

"Why is this little girl coming to me David? Do you think she had anything to do with my Dad?"

"Well, I guess that's why we're here. To find out what happened."

Viv looked in both directions but the little girl had disappeared.

"Let's go back to the hotel, I think you've had more

than enough fun for one day."

Though Viv was tired from the journey, she knew the little girl was not a figment of her imagination. Her perspective of life had been shifted to such a degree that nothing seemed impossible any more.

Darkness fell quickly. Heaven's sleepy veil dropped onto the Californian sky in an instant. Midnight had arrived before 10.30pm. Dinner consisted of two ham sandwiches, a large packet of cheesy puffs – a combination of sheer exhaustion and complete lack of imagination. It was only the excitement of the moment that kept them awake.

"What are you doing David?"

"Sketching."

"Why don't you watch television with me and be a complete couch potato?"

"It's a drawing for you."

"What is it?" she brightened enthusiastically.

"I'm visualising the little girl. She won't let me see her properly but she is showing me her eyes."

"Surely you can't remember a person from just their eyes?"

"That's all you need. The eyes are the window to the soul."

"I won't forget her face. I just can't understand why I keep seeing her?"

"She's trying to tell you something."

"What can I do to help her come to me again? Could you communicate with her?"

"I could but she knows you can put the puzzle together on your own. That is why she is coming to you."

David sat up and looked Viv straight in the eye.

"I'm going to give you some advice. Now that you're open to Spirit, you are going to get all kinds coming through."

"What do you mean, all kinds?"

"Not all Spirits are good, Viv."

"My Dad called them silent heroes, Spirits who are there to protect you."

"Of course, many are here to protect you. They are called your guides. They want the very best for you. But is every person walking on this earth, good?"

"Of course not."

"It's exactly the same in the Spirit world. So you need to protect yourself."

"Well, how can I do that?"

"If you repeat this little saying every day, you'll be fine."

"Shoot," she replied, realising she had caught onto a popular American colloquialism.

*'I surround myself with God's white light and only allow Higher Spirits to come into my aura.'*

Viv murmured it back to herself several times until she felt she had got the gist.

"It sounds a little silly," she giggled.

"Well, this silly little sentence will always keep you safe. The Spiritual plane is similar to here on earth. There are bad people and there are good people. Not everyone wants the best for you."

"So, why do these nasty Spirits give a hoot what these

Higher Spirits think, anyway? Surely they can break the rules?"

"The good are always higher than the bad. That is a universal truth."

David let out a big sigh and lay back on his bed, his shiny black hair flopping perfectly onto his eyes. Viv watched as his eyelids shut heavily. He was gone from the world in a moment.

◆

JOANNA SURVEYED the solid mahogany door and hoped she had made the right decision. She had been deliberating her sudden urge to express all to Doctor Cross, wondering whether it was an act of desperation or a genuine cry for help.

'I promised my Viv,' she consoled herself, the one thought that remained true in her mind.

"Mrs Goddard, if you'd like to follow me."

Joanna followed the young receptionist into the doctor's office.

"Joanna it's nice to see you again. I was expecting you last week."

"I had a lot on my mind," she frowned. "I'm sorry I missed the appointment."

"Please sit down."

Joanna kept her gaze fixed on Doctor Cross. She had never witnessed such perfection in a woman.

"Thank you. I'm a little under-dressed," Joanna announced, grimacing down at her stone washed jeans.

"I'm probably a little over dressed Joanna, force of habit."

"I wanted to talk about my daughter."

"How is Viv?"

"Fine, I think. She's gone to America for a while, with a friend, and I haven't heard from her since she left."

"She's probably having a wonderful time."

"The problem is that I have no idea when she's returning. This holiday is with a man old enough to know better. I don't know if he drinks, smokes, he could be a pot head for all I know..."

"Joanna, it's natural that you feel concerned, it's quite an adjustment when your grown daughter flies the nest for the first time, but you have to trust Viv."

"My daughter has become involved with the Spiritualist Church recently, I'm very frightened about the whole thing."

"Joanna, speaking from personal experience, I have been to a Spiritualist service. In fact, my daughter Rosie asked me to join her."

"What was it like?"

"For me it was an eye-opening experience. I was informed that my father wished to communicate with me."

"Surely it's all a con?"

"All I can say, Joanna, is that if the information I was given was all a lie, then they're the best in the business. There appears to be a lot out there that I don't know about yet. When I can take time out, I want to find out more for myself."

Joanna stood astonished. She felt totally sober.

◆

THE SUN streamed through the sea-blue curtains, it felt sticky already and the faint buzzing of the early morning traffic was a stimulating start to her morning. Viv had the morning papers from reception and laid them onto the bedspread. Her first contact would be the journalist at City News, in Los Angeles, who had covered her father's accident. She prayed that he would have all the answers.

"Good morning, City News. This is Mary-Ellen speaking. How may I help you?"

"Hello, may I speak to Guy Favor please?"

"What is the nature of your call ma'am?"

"Mr Favor wrote an article about my Dad over twelve months ago."

"Could you hold, please?"

Viv jumped as David drew back the curtains in one deft movement. She found herself gazing at his undeniably perfect silhouette. Had she not been jolted by the whining tones on the phone she would have been happy to stay in her state of delightful paralysis.

"Guy Favor."

"Oh hello. My name is Viv Goddard. I would like to speak to you about an article you wrote over twelve months ago."

"Geez, that's a long time ago but shoot."

"Well, you wrote a piece about my Dad, Simon Goddard."

"Sure, you're his kid. Gee, I'm sorry for your loss. If

there's anything I can do?"

The latter was easily the most insincere concern she had ever heard.

"Well, there is actually."

"This isn't gonna take too long is it?"

"I want you to take me through what happened."

"If you come to the headquarters my secretary will give you a copy of the article. Nice talking to you… Val is it?"

"Mr Favor? Mr Favor? David he just put the phone down on me."

David sat on the bed, drying his head vigorously with a towel. "Then you've got to go to the headquarters and make him listen."

"He was completely rude, to add insult to injury he actually forgot my name. I mean what kind of investigative journalist forgets a name in the space of twenty seconds?"

"The kind of journalist that works for City News."

"Could we go there this morning?" she pleaded sweetly.

"Sure," he replied, as he reached for a black linen shirt, draped over the back of the chair.

"A little warm to be wearing black again?" she ventured.

"It's light. By the way, how did that little sentence work out for you?"

"I must have repeated it about seven times last night. I was convinced something was behind our curtains."

"I think that was the god of the wind," he smiled.

Rena took a deep breath and knocked twice on Doctor Humphries' door. She hoped that she wouldn't be disturbing a tutorial.

"Come in!"

The growl lingered long after he had finished his retort. As she opened the door apprehensively, she understood why her fellow students called him the Big Bad Bear. He was imposing all right and had a brown beard more wild and confusing than a crow's nest. How did his wife kiss him? The very thought made her wince as she stood timidly, waiting for him to surface.

"I can come back at a more convenient time sir?"

"It's never convenient young woman. Now sit down and I will be with you when I have finished this paragraph. The most boring thing I have ever read but I'm going to finish it! This chapter is part of your next assignment. Good luck."

Rena forced a smile, the smell of cigars was evident, and it repulsed her. She wondered if she should refresh him on rule no.102 in the student handbook, no smoking on campus, which included staff.

"Finished. How can I assist you? Is it the 2,500 word essay I've set? If I've said it once I've said it a thousand times, 1,500 words is not acceptable."

"No Doctor Humphries, my query isn't work-related."

"Oh, then what is it?" he frowned, adjusting his glasses, which seemed to be tangled up in his hair.

"I've come to you because I'm not sure who I have to talk to. I want to leave the course."

"Do you mean switch to another course?"

"No, I want to leave university altogether."

"Well, that is a completely different kettle of fish. You've just started the course. The beard hasn't put you off, has it?"

"No, sir. Your beard is fine."

"Literature isn't quite what you expected?"

"I just don't think it is the course for me. If I'm honest with you, I prefer to read literature, and the thought of dissecting it for three years seems an endless amount of time to do something I don't enjoy."

"I should be convincing you, with every inch of this beard, for you to give it time, but I'm afraid I don't agree with that theory. If a course feels wrong, then it is, but why the drastic move to leave university altogether?"

"I need some time to think through what I really want to do."

"What would you like to do?"

"I'd like to paint with my Mum. I'd like to learn something which isn't tested by an examining board."

"You do realise that university isn't compulsory? There are other options young people take; they're called gap years. I'm sure you have a friend who's out there somewhere having an adventure before she makes a decision on what she wants to do with her life?"

"Actually, I do."

The City News headquarters was an imposing forty-storey building that dominated the downtown Los Angeles skyline. This place didn't have the breezy carefree vibe of Santa Monica. Viv could feel that this was a place of serious workers, most likely the kind of people who wouldn't have time for a story that was now 'old news'.

"You look pensive, Viv?"

"I am. What if he simply won't speak to me?"

"When he sees you, how could he refuse?"

David opened the door for her. "I'll be waiting for you by the car in an hour."

"You're not coming with me?"

"You don't need me with you. You're a smart, independent woman. There's nothing I can do to help you."

Viv moved with trepidation. David didn't budge until Viv had reached the floral centrepiece of the magnificent lobby. She whipped around but her companion was nowhere in sight. Viv moved closer, intoxicated by the smell of lilies. Pulling back her loose hair she sniffed in the aroma. It wasn't a particularly pretty smell but then the best smells on earth aren't always pretty.

"Can I help you ma'am?"

"Hello. I was just admiring this arrangement. It's really beautiful."

"Yes, it is," she said admiringly, looking on with great pride.

"My Dad used to bring my Mum lilies but she was always paranoid about them staining the carpet. She loved them all the same, still does."

"It's a small price to pay for such beautiful flowers," she said. Viv looked over to the lady's workstation where the phone had started ringing.

"I think that's your phone."

"I'll be with you in one minute," she cooed and wiggled over to her station. The woman's fragrance lingered next to her side, it was a nice place to be.

"I'm sorry about that, the second I move the phone always goes," the pretty blonde sighed cheerily. She reminded Viv of her Mum but without the stress lines.

"Are you Mary-Ellen?"

"Yes, I am. And you are?"

"My name is Viv Goddard. I called earlier this morning to speak to Guy Favor."

"Of course I remember, it's your English accent that makes you stand out. Do you have a meeting with Mr Favor?"

"I don't, if I'm honest with you, he was a little abrupt with me. I was really hoping I might be able to talk to him in person. It's regarding an article he wrote about my Dad."

"I could try for you Viv, but without an appointment..."

"I understand. Could you try though?" Viv added hopefully.

With lightening quick hands she dialled a four-digit number and in a matter of seconds was connected.

"Mr Favor, I have Viv Goddard at reception for you. She called earlier this morning. Uh-huh, oh dear. Well, she did fly all the way from England to see you."

Mary-Ellen shot Viv a knowing glance. "Thank you, Mr Favor."

"Will he see me?"

"He will, if you take a seat, he'll be down in a moment."

"Thank you so much. I like the bit about the flight to see him specially."

"Believe me hon', when it comes to men like Mr Favor they like to feel important. Don't tell him I said that though."

Viv was too nervous to sit down and kept her place by the flowers. She watched tentatively as the elevator doors parted and a short, fat, bald man made his way over to her.

"Are you Viv Goddard? Nice to meet you, I'm Guy Favor. I've only got twenty minutes. How about coffee?"

The verbal bullets kept coming at Viv, she had yet to acknowledge who she was.

"I've got a copy of the newspaper with me. Let's go."

"Okay," she agreed breathlessly.

"I guess this heat's a little hard for you to get used to?"

Viv had to force herself not to tell him that he was the one who seemed to be struggling. The handkerchief, attached to his brow, was beginning to drip.

"It makes a nice change from English weather actually."

"I wouldn't know; never been to England."

If he did she was certain he'd save a fortune on handkerchiefs.

"There's a coffee shop just around the block."

Viv felt the same oppressive heat which was plaguing Guy's head. The sleeves of her white top seemed to have merged with her skin, and a hot cup of coffee was the last thing on her mind.

"They serve the best coffee in the city. The espressos are nothing short of rocket fuel. I'm guessing you'll have tea."

His emphasis being on the tea made Viv wonder how many more stereotypical views of English people he had up his sleeve.

"Why would you say that?"

"You're English, don't you drink tea?"

"Water is fine."

Guy leaned over the counter to give the order, Viv found a table at the back of the darkened shop, the air conditioning provided welcome relief. As he came over she felt her nerves become more real, it was as if she was attending a job interview. She had one opportunity to get him on her side, she couldn't mess it up.

"One water. Now," he settled into his chair and took a small sip from his cup, "You're Simon Goddard's daughter and have come to ball me out over my article."

"No, I just want to ask some questions."

"Fine. Then shoot."

"Why would you think I was angry?"

"When it comes to covering fatal accidents a lot of families believe that you have more to say, or that you can explain everything that happened. Sometimes they just want someone to swing for what happened. They don't realise that accidents happen. Your father died as a result of speeding and skidding his motorcycle. There were no other parties involved."

"Well I do know it was an accident. I was more interested in finding out what you found out."

"Well," he took another sip. "I do know that while he was over here he took many trips up the coast. On the day of the accident he was headed to Monterey."

"Had he booked into a hotel?"

"No. I presumed it was spontaneous. His excursions corresponded with his days off. Nothing mysterious there. According to my notes he stopped over at Carmel, Monterey several times, even as far north as Mendocino, all scenic towns and popular tourist spots. I guess the motorcycle was a novelty option of travelling."

"You're right. It was his dream to own a Harley and I presume hiring was the next best thing. Did you speak to any of his friends?"

"Yeah, a guy named Mike Drake. He lives in Irvine, he filled me in on your Dad's trips."

"I know Mike, he used to come over to our house when I was little. He was at my Dad's funeral."

"Mike was closest to your father while he was over here. I think he'll be more of a help than I am."

"I really appreciate you seeing me."

He took a last sip and got up from his seat.

"I have a meeting in ten minutes. Mike Drake is your best bet."

"Wait, I don't have his phone number or address."

"Here!"

Ripping half of his notes in two, he placed a crinkled piece of paper onto Viv's lap.

"Good luck to you, miss."

Guy had promised twenty minutes but had left by the eighth. He had fulfilled his part of the bargain however and had given her what she needed. But the absence of chitchat had left a gaping hole in her schedule. It left a problem of what to do for the remainder of the hour.

'I'll just walk, it's not as pretty as the beach but it's a great city,' she thought to herself.

The street came to a junction, she had the option of turning left or taking the mammoth crossing. As she made her way left she saw a sight that she hadn't counted on seeing. She couldn't be certain, but if her eyes served her well David was leaning against a wall, coffee in hand, talking to an extremely attractive blonde woman. She decided to turn away and would wait, as planned, by the car. She still had twenty-five minutes to go.


"So what happened with the journalist? Was he any help?" David asked.

"He told me to contact Mike Drake. He was a friend. Where is Irvine by the way?"

"It's in Orange County, about a half-hour drive from LA."

"Apparently Mike lives there, it would be good if we could talk to him. Today, tomorrow," she hesitated. "Whenever. So, what did you get up to, anything nice?"

"I didn't do anything, I just hung around, had a coffee. In fact, I met someone for coffee. I'd like to tell you about it when we get back to the hotel."


The chilled hotel room was a veritable sanctuary from the soaring temperatures outside.

"David," she puffed, fanning herself with the nearest

newspaper available. "I have to confess that I saw you with a woman. I presume that is the person you met for coffee?"

"You are the detective!" he sounded impressed. "I hope we didn't give the wrong impression? We're not a couple, at least we're not any more."

This piece of news needed clarifying.

"Why were you hanging around with an ex-girlfriend?"

David perched on the end of the bed and seemed to be struggling with the opening sentence.

"This is probably going to sound unusual."

"Well, nothing on this trip could be described as usual."

"Shannen's in serious trouble. I was told by a fellow Medium at church a month back."

"What kind of trouble?"

"You have to realise that I came to England to get away from the life I had with Shannen. We both come from wealthy families, and up until a few years ago my days were spent partying with a group of other rich kids, including Shannen. She can't see that the path she has taken will destroy her."

"So what do you have to do?"

"I've been told that she will come into danger. I will know the place as soon as I get into contact with her."

"And where will that be?"

"At a party. I thought of the word 'party' as soon as I saw her. Oddly enough the parties we had were always in Irvine."

Beads of sweat were beginning to roll off Viv's brow. It

seemed that discovering her father's path was becoming entangled with the paths of others. Strangely, she felt a pang of jealously at the thought of spending time with an attractive female counterpart, though it wasn't in Viv's nature to turn away from a cry of help. Witnessing David's genuine concern made her warm to the idea.

"I think that's very noble of you. If your path is to help her, then that is what we're going to do. I need to see Mike in Irvine and you need to help Shannen in Irvine. It will be like killing two birds with one stone, so to speak."

Viv had given the go ahead for David to contact Shannen again. While he made use of the telephone at reception, Viv had the chance to contact Mike and his wife, Sally, in the hope they would welcome an impromptu visit. She remembered they used to bring a huge bag of sweets when they visited her parents. Because they had no children of their own, Viv liked to believe she was their surrogate daughter.

"Hello, Drake residence?" Sally opened with clipped tones.

"Sally is that you? This is Viv Goddard."

"Oh my goodness Viv! Oh, how lovely to hear your voice."

"It's so nice to hear yours."

"How are you my darling?"

"I'm fine. You'll never guess where I am."

"You don't mean to say you're in the States? Where are you? California? With your mother?"

"I'm in California but not with Mum. I'm with a friend.

Sally, could I come and see you?"

"Viv you are welcome to come over anytime."

"Is today okay?"

"Of course it is. That's marvellous."

"Will Mike be in too?"

"Yes, he's on his way back from a business trip, he should be here late this afternoon. I know he would love to see you. Oh sweetie I've missed you. Do you have a pen as you'll need our address?"

"I already have it."

"I can't wait to see you sweetheart. Bring your friend, won't you."


As Viv leaned over the balcony railings and breathed in the sea air, she understood why her father called this his perfect beachside town. She was sure that she would return time and time again, just like he had done.

"Don't lean too far over!" David warned.

"I'm alright. I'm keeping a look out for Shannen."

Viv hadn't needed a brief on her appearance, Shannen was already crystal clear in her memory. At that very moment, she spied a blonde hurrying towards the hotel entrance.

"She's here."

Viv watched as David hesitated, he took a bite out of his candy bar and frantically made an attempt to make the bed.

"What are you doing?"

"Making the bed. I gave her our number so she'll be on her way up now."

"Great!" Viv replied, rather too excited to be believable.

Viv stood glumly by the dresser. A knock on the door came moments later.

"You're being great about this. If you're not an angel then I don't know who is."

"Angel?" she questioned.

Viv stole a brief glance in the mirror; her hair just perfect, awaiting this meeting. She knew she looked good as the excitable blonde entered their hotel room.

"Hey baby. I missed ya," Shannen cooed and threw perfectly tanned arms over his shoulders. David politely refrained as he made the introductions.

"Shannen, this is my friend, Viv Goddard. Viv, this is Shannen Tully."

"Hello Shannen."

"Nice to meet you Viv," she whined, "Wow, you're so white!"

"Just blame it on the English weather."

"Ha!"

And in one plastic gesture both girls exchanged fake laughs, so loud it would have been impolite not for David to join in, and he did. Viv had whooped for England, it made her feel false. Viv made a mental note not to think bad thoughts about this woman who had made an unflattering comment about the pallor of her skin, after all, this was a woman who was in supposed danger.

"Lunch ladies?"

"I just ate," Shannen piped.

"Actually, I would like some lunch," Viv intervened.

Viv grabbed her purse and headed out of the door. Once out of earshot, Shannen made her appraisal.

"She's pretty David, a little young for you though."

"So, you've eaten already?"

"Now, you don't get off so easily. What's going on between the two of you and don't tell me nothing?"

"Nothing. Let's go eat. The restaurant downstairs should still be serving. They do a great brunch."

"I'll find out David. I always do."

Even the prospect of eggs, sunny side up, couldn't hide Viv's concern, this woman didn't appear like the sort David would go for. Viv had a bad feeling about her, as if she knew this was a person who wouldn't change no matter how much David was prepared to try and help her.

"So, let me get this straight. You're on some sort of spiritual mission to see what happened to your father?"

"Not exactly. I know how my Dad died. I just feel there are some gaps to fill in."

"To get some closure?"

"Sure," Viv agreed, unclear on what 'closure' actually meant.

"David you're pretty quiet. Is your ex-girlfriend and your current making you nervous?"

"I beg your pardon?" Viv blurted, orange juice dribbling down her chin.

"God, I love her. She's so English!"

"What do you mean by current?"

"It was a joke. I was teasing David earlier about you two being an item."

Silence ensued. As David looked over to see why the eggs were taking so long, Shannen leaned in towards Viv.

"He's so edgy. He's usually so relaxed."

"I wouldn't know," Viv looked away, fixating on a group of rollerbladers outside, so as not to come off as too rude.

"Just so you know, he never used to be like this."

The eggs arrived just in time.

"So, while you're here I'm going to make the most of you two. There's a pool party that's started just about now."

"Party?" David questioned, his inner fear had been realised.

"Amanda Peterson's party to be exact. Viv, out here we party all the time. And you're both coming with me, right after the eggs. It's all settled. You'll come over after your… where is it you have to go?"

"To see friends of my Dad's."

"Oh. Well, you'll need some cheering up after that one."

Shannen managed to induce severe indigestion, in both of them.

"David, after brunch, why don't you go and check out? I'll go upstairs to pack. There's no point staying another night; we don't know how long we'll be with Mike and Sally in Irvine."

"That's a good idea. We could always stay at a Best Western or a Hampton Inn."

"Hey! There won't be any staying in hotels. You'll both be too busy partying."

The idea of spending the entire night with Shannen was too awful to contemplate. However, Viv realised that David had been right about the party. She braced herself for the events to come.

Viv had been relegated to the back seat and was being taken, very much against her better judgement, to a pool party in Irvine. The sea breeze was long gone. Viv pushed her face against the half open window to catch some air.

"You're so English, honey, wind up the window. We're in the land of air-conditioning now."

David glanced in the mirror and caught Viv's disgruntled expression. She was being mocked. His reassuring wink made the journey bearable.

"Maybe you're too Californian," he added.

"David!" she gasped. "Was that a witty contribution from you? You've really changed."

"Have I changed in your opinion, Shannen?"

"Totally. For one, you used to be out of your head most of the time."

"What does that mean?" Viv spoke up.

"It means your travel companion was always stoned."

"Thanks Shannen," David said through gritted teeth.

Shannen's waif-like frame slid surreptitiously down her seat, as if she were oblivious to the embarrassment she had just caused.

"Did I say something wrong?"

David's concentration was fixed on the horizon; his stony expression wasn't showing any sign of letting up.

For the moment, it was turning out to be a good day.

Shannen was as blunt as a spoon and David couldn't have been more angered by her remarks. If Shannen kept this behaviour going, Viv was sure her bikini would never see the light of day, packed away safe in her suitcase, which is exactly where she wanted it to remain.

"This is one thing you have to know about David, Viv. He's as moody as hell. I'm sure you've noticed."

"Sometimes, but everyone gets moody."

Shannen tilted her blonde head to the side and gave Viv one of her blinding smiles.

"You're diplomatic, I'll give you that. Your very controlled, polite, British facade will fall away once I get you to this party. It's going to be one hell of a night, I can feel it. What route are you taking David?" Shannen turned.

"Route 1, it's really pretty along the coast."

"No, no, take the 405, Route 1 will take all day, I want to party," said Shannen forcefully.

David obliged just to avoid an argument. What's a 'rowt' thought Viv, but stayed quiet just like David.


Viv felt her legs come back to life as they walked through the apartment complex where Mike and Sally lived. The perfectly manicured communal area and whitewashed buildings gave a very Mediterranean feel to the Californian climes.

"What a cute place. It's like a little Spanish village."

David had wandered off in front, while Shannen had rather inappropriately linked arms with Viv.

"You know what?"

"What?"

"You've got a great chest, why do you wear tops that cover them up so much? You'll attract David a lot easier if you show it off."

"Excuse me?" she broke away, "David's my friend, I'm not on this trip to… seduce him."

"Whatever honey. I've seen the way you look at him. And I've seen how protective you are of him. What would you call it?"

"Friendship."

"Is that what they're calling it nowadays? And by the way, apartment 201 is on the right."

As Viv headed in David's direction she could see how distracted he had become, his mind was definitely preoccupied.

"It's the party isn't it?" Viv offered. "It's going to happen at the party?"

David nodded solemnly, and linked her arm as they continued on Shannen's trail.

"My darling little Vivvy! Sweetheart, it's wonderful to see you."

"It's even better to see you. You changed your hair," Viv enthused.

"It was about time I had a change," she giggled.

"Sally, this is Shannen. Shannen, my friend Sally Drake."

"You must be Viv's travelling companion, lovely to meet you."

"Well, I'm her companion for the day. I'm a friend of David's actually."

David had been loitering at the back of the friendly commotion, and had no intention of stepping up without an introduction. Shannen stepped back and revealed the quiet man, who extended his arm politely.

"Sally, this is my travelling companion, David Lancer," Viv smiled proudly.

"It's a pleasure, David."

"It's great to meet you. You live in a really cool place I have to say."

"Well, thank you very much. It keeps the beating sun off our heads. Now come in the three of you, you must be parched."

The layout inside was clean and bright, the tiled floor and the white walls made everything seem cooler than it was. The scent of jasmine from a large pot-pourri bowl in the centre of the room gave a very British feel to the house. Both Sally and her mother, embarrassingly enough, used to make their own pot-pourri, the thought made her think of home and her mother.

"I laid a few snacks in the kitchen. I wasn't sure what time to expect you."

As Shannen and David pulled up a couple of bar stools at the table, Viv found herself looking at a picture on Sally's fridge.

"I call that my memory board."

"The picture's great, I haven't seen it before."

"Your Dad and Mike were at Malibu beach. Ron called them chickens for not going in for a dip. I think it was a certain shark film that put your Dad and Mike off," she chuckled.

"Only the English take that film so seriously. Come on, you're in California, you have to go for a swim," Shannen couldn't stop herself from talking even when her mouth was full. She had a half-eaten sandwich in her mouth, David comically shut it for her, which Sally found amusing.

Viv watched, as the sun-drenched kitchen highlighted the golden streaks in Sally's red hair. Her curvy figure had become rounder since the funeral, but she was still the Sally that Viv remembered so well. Her accent was the purest she had heard in a while, not in the least bit affected by her American sojourn.

"Believe it or not that jug contains real lemonade, I made it this morning. Do you like lemonade, David?"

"Like lemonade? I love lemonade."

Sally graciously poured three glasses full and managed to keep a gentle conversation flowing throughout, she was the perfect hostess.

"I must mention now that Mike isn't here at the moment."

"Is he still due this afternoon?" Viv hoped.

"I had no way of contacting you. It was such short notice. Mike called earlier and told me he will be back tomorrow morning."

Viv felt her knees almost keel in, it wasn't the thought of spending one more day in Irvine but the prospect of even more time with Shannen.

"You're all welcome to stay the night. I have a spare room and plenty of pillows and duvets."

"That's really kind of you Sally."

"Yeah, that is kind, but there will be no need, they're coming to a pool party."

"Well that sounds fun. A lot more enjoyable than beers and a TV movie, which is what I had planned."

That was exactly what Viv needed – beer and a night in front of the box.

A familiar and yet contorted sound emanated from what appeared to be Shannen's crotch. This caused a momentary burst of excitement on Shannen's behalf before the ring was mercifully answered.

"Amanda! Baby! Yeah, we're here. He's fine, moodier though. She's so English! We're on our way, have three beers ready. Bye! Guys that was Amanda."

"We'd never have guessed," David responded dryly.

"The party's begun!"


The three-bedroom house backed onto a large piece of land, which was bumper to bumper filled with cars. Piles of garbage sacks littered their pathway.

"It's filthy. Jesus, I've got crap all over my new shoes."

This pleased Viv no end.

"Shannen, are we going to a party for rodents?" David enquired in all sincerity.

"Don't get sarcastic with me. You've partied at this house more than me." Shannen scorned, as she scraped the remnants of a rotting banana skin on the edge of Amanda's tired old fence.

"Hey girlfriend!" a diminutive brunette cried. Her small freckly face looked perfectly sweet in the sunlight as she embraced her friend. Her demonic grip on three huge beer bottles indicated to Viv that this was the infamous party girl. "Well, well. Mr Lancer has returned. I knew you couldn't keep away for too long."

"Missed you too much. Amanda, this is my good friend Viv."

"Great to meet one of David's English friends," she leant forward and air-kissed her left cheek. "You look very sweet, but boy are you pale. We're going to get a little sun on you this afternoon. Here," she passed Viv one of the bottles. "Drink up. There's plenty of partying to be done."

With one sip Viv had been ushered into a backyard of drink and debauchery. If her eyes had not mistaken her, the over-sized pool contained a plethora of glistening, albeit naked bodies.

"Forgive my friends Viv. They're a little wild. I promise, going topless is not mandatory."

Over in the far corner of the garden a fearsome barbecue was ablaze, milling around it was a crowd of hungry looking people. She felt the small of her back being gently squeezed as David leant over her shoulder.

"You okay? If Amanda chews your ear off, come and find me."

"Why, where are you going?"

"To see an old friend, Zach. He's manning the barbecue or at least trying to. I won't be long," he kissed her softly on the cheek, before he stepped over tanning bodies to his friend.

"I think he walks like a geek but I never told him that," Viv whispered to Amanda.

"That's due to an injury. Falling off his bike too many times. I'm surprised he can walk to tell you the truth. You know what, I think you're very cute."

Viv was taken aback, this perky party girl was fast becoming a welcome replacement from Shannen.

"Thanks. You too."

"Now, as Shaz has disappeared, come clean. What's the deal with you and David, are you fucking?"

"What? No, no, of course not, we're just friends."

"I don't believe it. A cute guy like that, don't you even want to?"

"No, he's my friend. I don't think of him that way."

"Sure," her nonplussed response seemed to linger as she wandered off towards Shannen. Viv was left on her own, her worst nightmare had been realised. As she scoured the crowds to see where the petite Amanda had gone off to, it became clear that she would have to make some effort.

"Hey, I'm Krista! You're David's girl right? Amanda told me to come and say hi."

Viv was fast feeling like the pity case of this little soiree.

"Thanks for coming over. I wasn't sure what to do with myself."

"Want to go for a dip?"

"I haven't brought a costume," she lied.

"Well that's not a problem."

"Actually, I'm just going to finish my drink."

"I'll join you. Want to go and sit down?"

"You read my mind. The sun is baking."

"You're probably not used to this weather. I hang out

in the sun all of the time."

Two precarious looking deckchairs shaded by an over-sized umbrella, were just what Viv wanted.

"How do you know David then, Krista?"

"We hung around in a big group in High School. Last time I saw David was at a party just like this; next thing we heard he had moved to England. Everyone thought it was so weird."

An innocent and naive approach would probably coax the vital information Viv had yet to gain regarding David's past.

"So, why did he move?" she edged in closer.

"I suppose it was to do with his father, they never got on. Things got worse after his mother died."

"But David's father died also?"

"Oh, so he's playing it that way. Listen Viv, I don't know what lies he's been feeding you but his father is definitely alive. Don't look so shocked. Don't tell me a guy's never lied to you before?"

"What does his father do then? Does he live in California?"

"He sure does. A goddamn multi-millionaire to boot. Ever heard of City News in Los Angeles? That's all his!"

◆

IT HADN'T occurred to Joanna not to drink. Doctor Cross had yet to address her alcoholism and was therefore temporarily off the hook. So she settled down for an evening of drink and eventual inebriation.

"This is good. Time for myself. No-one to answer to, this is really good," she smiled and poured herself an over-generous gin and tonic. As she sipped in the quietness of her living room, with only herself for company, she decided a false sense of security and companionship was better than nothing, and switched on the television for the first time in a very long while. As she channel-hopped, it was evident she had not missed much and stretched over to the video cabinet to see what it had to offer.

'Mr Wayne, I haven't seen you for a while', she smirked to herself, holding the box set in her hand. She still wondered why Viv made such a fuss over this old actor. As a seven-year old she would watch his old films time and time again. It was unusual, but then she expected nothing less from her daughter. She threw the box down and made a mental note to throw them out the following morning.

The news had acted as a wake up call to Viv. David's past had been glossed over up until this point and it was clear there were hidden secrets beginning to surface.

Krista had long since wandered off. A series of half-naked young women inebriated, up to their eyeballs, had passed Viv many times. They asked teasing questions just to mock her English voice and her pale legs. She was the token freak. Two tepid bottles of beer later she felt the courage to wander across the lawn in an attempt to find David. The late afternoon hue caused the dwellers to wane. Most lay asleep on the grass and in her way.

The back door was open, though no-one was in the

kitchen. It stank of lager and the feeble appetisers laid out on the island unit did little to entice her appetite.

"Want a beer?"

Viv swivelled round to see who had walked up on her suddenly.

"Actually, I was just looking for David Lancer."

"I think he's in the pool room. Are you sure you don't want a drink?"

"Why not, I'll have another beer. I'm Viv by the way."

"I'm Tony, an old friend of David's."

Tony was not only an old friend of David's but also an extraordinary tall one at that. Though that wasn't the only distracting thing about Tony, his Mohican was quite a head turner.

"I play guitar in a band. It's okay but we're getting better."

Viv nodded graciously.

"Well, it must take time. It's nice to meet you but I think I had better find David."

As she edged her way out of the door she felt the nagging sensation that she was being rude. Tony slouched against the fridge and nodded with indifference. She turned back.

"I'm sure he'll come and find me when he's finished the game. Do you mind if I sit with you?"

"Sure," he brightened and politely offered her a chair. "Are you and David going together?"

"Not to my knowledge. We're friends."

"That's alright then. He and Shannen are having a heated conversation in the pool room. I didn't know if they were getting back together."

Viv swallowed hard, and tried to keep her expression the same as prior to this uncomfortable revelation.

"We could go and catch the last few rays, plus you haven't had an Anthony special, yet."

"A what?"

"I'm a legend on the barbecue. It's an all meat sandwich, grilled to perfection by yours truly. Come on, I'll make you one."

Viv happily followed; Tony was turning out to be her only ally, and it didn't look like David was about to make an appearance any time soon.


Shannen slammed her pool cue onto the green felt. The game was merely a pretext, she wanted some answers and she wanted them now.

"Here's the million dollar question. Why did you leave, David?"

David placed his cue down and took a swig of beer before he responded.

"I was tired of the life I had here."

"With me?"

"All of it Shannen. Do you realise that the same people who were at my last party are at this party! The same crowd, smoking the same spliffs, gorging the same beer."

"And parties are offensive to you?"

"It's the people. I was becoming the bonehead party boy who did nothing with his life. All of our friends are still living off Daddy's credit card, most of them are about to turn thirty. Aren't the alarm bells going off yet? I wanted to see if you had changed, if you had made a life of your own."

"No you haven't. Basically you've come here to ruin this party and to make me feel bad about myself."

"Shannen I want to help you. If you continue on this path it's going to destroy you. You don't have to live like this."

"I'm afraid I'm going to have to interrupt this little pep talk with a few words of my own. Here it is from me to you. This is my life, David. Not yours!" And she stormed off.

"You don't like it do you?"

"Maybe if I had some ketchup it would be more palatable. Or maybe because you've given me a loaf and six sausages!"

"Are you mocking the Anthony special?"

"I wouldn't dream of it," she giggled.

Viv was beginning to feel more at ease with this stranger than she had anticipated. They had taken two deck chairs up by the pool as the party had now moved into the house. Viv tilted her head back and gazed at the hazy pink sky above.

"You're really lucky having this beautiful weather. Do you have a lot of parties here?"

"We party here about every two weeks."

"The last time I had a party was when I was ten. My Mum made blue jelly."

"That's jello to us. I used to love it when I was a kid."

"I've never seen blue jelly since," Viv moaned.

"Do you live with your parents, Viv?"

"I live with my Mum."

"Cool. What about your old man?"

"My Dad died over a year ago."

"I'm really sorry. There we were having a good time and I screw it up. Do you want to go inside?"

"I'm actually just enjoying being here."

"I'll be back in one moment. I have to use the little boy's room."

"How romantic."

"I'll be back."

After a long twenty minute wait, it was evident Tony wasn't coming back so Viv reluctantly decided to rejoin the party. The three groups of the party had finally merged as one. Firstly 'the bedroom gang', aka, the dope fiends, who were now gathered in the sitting room playing a drunken and dirty version of spin the bottle. Secondly 'the bikini babes' who were being dried off from their late swimming session by their respective partners, quite literally, in the middle of the sitting room. Lastly, 'the non-belonger' – Viv – who was attempting to make coherent conversation to a very stoned Amanda.

"Amanda, have you seen David?"

"Viv, you're the sweetest chick I've ever met!" she yelped.

"Thanks but have you seen David?"

"Someone mention my name?"

David crouched next to Viv and warmly pulled her close.

"I was beginning to think you'd left."

"I'm sorry, I tried to talk to her."

"And?"

"She didn't want to hear anything. I still have a feeling that something isn't right though."

"Where is she now?"

"Talking to a guy named Tony."

That explained his absence, though she wasn't about to admit that her party companion had ditched her for someone prettier and notably blonder.

"Come on you two. How about spin the bottle?"

David politely opted out of spin the bottle much to the annoyance of the hostess.

"You have to! Please, please, please!" Amanda whined.

"Maybe later," his mind was already preoccupied.

Amanda lost immediate interest with the argument and began to snuggle up to a geeky looking man, totally involved in his video game.

"I'm going to find her."

Viv was promptly on David's trail. She had already lost him once and wasn't about to lose him for the second time. He approached a young guy and sought his assistance.

"Hey Tommy, have you seen Shannen around?"

"I saw her leave with Tony. I think," he slurred.

"You're kidding. Where did they go?"

"Would you quit with the questions, you're ruining my buzz." Tommy fell over and made no attempt to get up.

Viv peered through the window. The same dull ache she experienced the night her father died plagued her entire being. Everything was still in the garden, apart from a solitary bush at the end of the lawn. She drew closer, pressing her face against the glass. The bush started to shake, at first she thought it might be the breeze, though she noticed something behind the bush and the frantic shaking led her out of the house to the precise location which had demanded her attention. She placed her hand atop the prickly leaves and looked closer.

"Hello?" Viv ventured, at first glance there didn't seem to be anybody there.

A figure materialised in front of Viv's eyes. She could not go closer for fear the little girl might run away again. Viv watched her stretch out her arm and with a painted pink fingertip, point in the direction of the nearby street. Viv had no idea at that moment where this was leading.

"Little girl, what you are trying to say?"

She only smiled and skipped along the street, turned the corner and was gone.

"Viv, what are you doing out here?"

"The little girl came to me David, she pointed in that direction," Viv re-enacted the little girl's exact movement. "David you have to think what that meant, I have a feeling it's to do with Shannen."

David kept very still and allowed his mind to wander. Shannen was at the centre of his thoughts but she wasn't alone.

"The park," he said suddenly. "The little girl was pointing in the direction of the park. Viv stay here."

David remembered the street by heart, and the park would take him only seconds at the speed at which he was now running. A dark shadow was cast over his thoughts as he leapt over the metal railings where sounds of a scuffle drew near. The playground stood empty. As David surveyed the surrounding area, a cluster of bushes began to rustle violently.

"Shannen!" he yelled.

David's body tensed fiercely. He knew instinctively that it was Shannen in the bushes, he knew this was the moment that began his mission. Fear consumed him, but anger thrust him explosively forward. He sped towards the bushes hoping beyond hope that she was okay. Shannen's slender frame fell to the ground as David powered through the bush. His trembling hands grabbed a crouching figure.

"What did you do to her?" David yelled, grabbing him by the collar.

"We were only having a little fun."

"I thought you were a friend?" David strained, he looked to Tony for an explanation. Tony shrugged with indifference. At that moment David allowed nature rather than reason to take over and with one blow Tony fell to the ground.

"What did he do to you?" With every word David shook violently, he stuttered as he felt his anger peak, "How did he hurt you?"

David stroked Shannen's face, her lip had been cut, and her pale pink top had been ripped revealing a soiled bra.

"He kept hitting me. I fell off the swing and he grabbed me," she quivered. "I managed to break away but he dragged me to the bushes. I want to get out of here," she panicked. "David get me out!"

"You're safe. Nothing can hurt you now."

He held her close, squeezing her tightly – relief drained through his body. Shannen was frightened but she had escaped intact.

Viv remained on the front lawn. It was a relief to have some distance from the revellers who were well into the party mood again. She stretched out her legs on the grass and allowed her mind to wander. Her eyes suddenly fixed on a dark figure, slowly making his way towards the house. Viv leapt up instantly. David was carrying Shannen.

"Viv, go and find a free bedroom. Quick," he shouted over.

She darted inside the house; the party was now in full swing.

"Hey Viv! Come and play spin the bottom. Ethan's never kissed a British chick before."

"Amanda, we need a bedroom."

"You've scored already?" Amanda rolled with laughter. Viv would have more luck talking to a brick wall.

She bolted up the stairs and opened the first door she came to.

"Hello, is anyone in here?"

The coast was clear. Viv fluffed the pillows and drew back the blanket as David pushed through the doorway with Shannen in his arms. He lowered her gently, pulling the sheets right up to her chin, swaddling her shaking limbs.

"What happened to Shannen?"

"I should have known. I waited too long. If it wasn't for you Viv I wouldn't have got there in time."

"Who did this to her?"

Viv perched on the edge of the bed and began stroking Shannen's hair, it was the one thing she did best. She had had plenty of practice with her mother.

"It was Tony."

"You must be mistaken. Tony is a nice guy. I should know, I was talking to him for most of the evening."

"Would a nice guy do this to a woman?"

"I don't understand," Shannen groaned, as she lifted her head. "We were laughing and joking and then he came on to me. I said 'no' and that's when he hit me."

"I'm calling the police."

"Viv, you can't. I couldn't stand the humiliation."

"Shannen, the guy attacked you. The police have to know, or else this guy is going to do the same to other girls."

"Fine. Just not tonight. I need you both to stay with me."

Viv was surprised she had used the word 'both', obviously the hair stroking had done the trick.

"I knew this was going to happen," David said quietly.

"What do you mean?"

"I knew you were going to get hurt tonight, I should have stayed with you all night."

"David, I know all about you and your spiritual beliefs. I realise you're some hot shot Medium where you live but don't pretend to play God."

"I'm not Shannen. I just know that the path you are taking is going to lead to more incidents like tonight. The people who you associate with are only going to drag you down."

"So is that why you left?" she demanded.

"Yes."

"This is how I live my life. I'm twenty-eight years old and I don't need you to play babysitter. In fact, I don't want either of you here tonight. Just leave."

They didn't leave, despite Shannen's protestations.

◆

HER EYES opened, heavy and sticky. Viv threw the blanket away from her clammy limbs. Even at this early hour, the heat was oppressive. Viv lay back down, careful not to wake Shannen, who she had shared a bed with that night. Viv moved closer to Shannen's face. The bruise on her left eye had become puffy and her lower lip had a deep red cut. She looked peaceful now. Viv leaned in closer and kissed her lightly on her forehead. The woman had been through a night of hell and she sincerely hoped everything would work out for her.

"Good morning."

Viv rolled out of bed and stumbled over to her companion, sitting by the window.

"What time is it?" she yawned.

"8am," he whispered gently.

The smell of a summer morning had penetrated through the half-open window, it was as if last night had never been.

"You saved Shannen, Viv. I couldn't have helped her if it hadn't been for you."

"I suppose we're like a double act. I'm the brains, you're the brawn," she joked. "Seriously David, we helped her together. I think it's up to her to do the rest. If this hasn't shown her that she has to make changes, I don't know what will." Viv glanced back in the hope Shannen hadn't woken.

"It's time to leave," David said quietly.

"We can't leave Shannen."

"We have to Viv. Like you said, it's up to her to do the rest."

Viv felt a pang of guilt as they gently closed the door behind them. As they descended the stairs the overwhelming stench of unwashed bodies and alcohol filled the air. Viv felt the sunshine sweep through her body as they emerged into the daylight. She felt fantastic. As David reversed out of the back yard, he looked up and caught a final glimpse of his ex. Shannen didn't cry or beat the window. She stood almost motionless, just gave a gentle wave. He tried to remember how she was, when she was happy. He recalled a time when they were fifteen; playing at their local park for hours after school until the sun set. They were no longer fifteen and she was no longer the Shannen he remembered so well.

"Don't look so solemn, you did try. If Shannen wanted to change her life she would have come away with us."

"I guess," he shrugged. "They're just a confused bunch

of rich kids, who spend their lives sniffing and screwing."

"Like in the Sixties."

"Yeah, but with less love."

"Do you love Shannen?"

"I thought I did. But coming here again made me realise that love when you're sixteen, and love when you're almost thirty, are completely different things."

Viv watched as the early morning traffic whizzed by, ordinary people frantically trying to get to work. It made her think of her own situation. When she returned home she would have to find a job, but for the present, there were more pressing matters at hand.

"David, I know your Dad never passed away. He's living in Los Angeles isn't he? Don't feel guilty, I know you must have your reasons for not telling me," she concluded.

"Who told you this?"

"Would it matter?"

"No. But who told you?"

"Krista, one of the girls at the party."

"What else do you know?"

"His name is Conrad."

"And?"

"He's the proprietor and editor in chief of City News in Los Angeles."

◆

RENA ARRIVED on her mother's doorstep at 8pm precisely. She had never been so nervous in her entire life. For the past week she had assured her mother that all was well at university, when in fact, she was making arrangements to leave her course.

"Rena? What are you doing home my darling?"

"Mum, I need to have a talk with you."

Carmen missed the tension in Rena's voice.

"Don't you have lectures tomorrow? Are you on reading week? I must pencil in when you have these holidays, so I can prepare. I don't have much food in..."

"Mum, listen for a moment."

Rena removed the cushions her mother had arranged at the corner of the sofa and sat down in their place.

"I'm not on reading week or exam week or any sort of a holiday, I've left my course."

"Pardon? Have you changed to another course?" she asked hopefully.

"No, I've left completely."

Carmen prided herself on being a liberal and an understanding parent, but she felt bewildered at the revelation.

"Mum, don't be angry."

"Rena, I'm shocked. I don't know what to make of this."

"I've never seen you like this Mum. Please look at me. Don't be cross."

"I'm not," she replied with perfect restraint. It might have occurred to her to have a more eloquent speech prepared, but at this time she feared what she might say if she did not remain quite still.

"I had to leave Mum. I felt miserable on campus, with

my room-mate and with the course. I've thought my decision through and I just know it was the right thing to do."

"You've only just started the course. You haven't given yourself time to make friends, or settle in," she whimpered.

"Mum, please don't be upset."

"Why did you feel you couldn't talk to me about it? I was here, thinking you were having the time of your life."

"Mum, that's just the thing. All my life I've tried to do everything to make other people happy."

"I've always told you Rena, that the only person you need to make happy is yourself."

"I know Mum, but I've always done everything to plan. I participated in every after-school activity, I studied non-stop. Do you remember that I used to revise on Christmas Eve? Now I have to make a few decisions of my own."

Carmen pulled her only daughter close.

"Mum, I'm not saying I never want to go back. I don't even know what I want to do for a living. I just chose a prestigious course in a prestigious university, to make the family proud. There was a reason I took those years out before university, I wasn't sure it was the right path for me."

"What would you like to do?"

"I've always had a desire to go travelling. Though I never really mentioned it."

"How would you fund it?" Carmen wondered, getting down to the practicalities.

"I saved a lot through working in my gap years and I've hardly touched my savings."

"Where would you go?"

"I was thinking of America."

"Thinking of reconciling with an old acquaintance?" Carmen wondered.

"I don't even know where Viv has gone but Joanna will. I miss my friend, I just need to do this."

"When are you planning on going?"

"As soon as possible."


Viv knocked three times. She did not feel the same flush of optimism she had done before. David stood two steps back.

"Look who it is? Come here you."

Viv flung her arms over Mike's broad shoulders. He was built as strong as a grisly bear.

"It's so great to see you again. Like the new look?"

"I can't believe you shaved your beard off," Viv laughed, her tension released in a flash.

"I can't either. I decided to make a change, the wife loves it."

"Yes she does," Sally smiled and ushered the reunion into the sitting room where chocolate cake had already been laid out. Viv took a moment to look upon her second Dad. Mike hadn't aged at all. He still had a mop of brown hair with only a couple of notable greys. His gentle manner soothed everyone he was around.

"How's my girl enjoying that cake?"

"It's the best thing I've ever tasted."

"We usually have a little girl called Casey around about now. Her mother can't afford a babysitter so she sits with me. I usually make her a chocolate cake," Sally smiled.

"Oh, I'm sorry," Viv dropped the sponge. "Are we eating Casey's cake?"

"Don't be silly. Casey's at her father's today but she would have loved to have met you. Wouldn't she Mike?"

"She certainly would."

"Tea anyone?"

As Sally scuttled off into the kitchen, Viv decided it would be the right time to confront Mike about her Dad.

"Mike, could I ask you some questions?"

Mike stiffened slightly and replied, "You can ask me anything you want."

"I just want to say one thing. Please don't hold back, to spare my feelings. I just want to know everything. For my peace of mind, you understand."

"What do you mean?"

"My Dad took trips along the coast. I found that out from a reporter who covered Dad's..." she paused, "Dad's story. I knew that Dad was closest to you while he was out here. Therefore, I know you know more than anybody else."

"I don't know how useful I'll be Viv. Your Dad kept quiet about a lot of things."

Sally came over with a pot of Earl Grey.

"Why did Dad take so many trips to the coast? Was it work-related? Did he have friends there?"

"He took a liking for the coast, it's very beautiful."

Mike was glossing over the truth, her father liked

travelling yes, but surely not to the same place over and over again.

"He liked Monterey particularly didn't he?"

"It's a beautiful place."

"I'm sure, but why so many times? Seriously, did he have friends? Maybe friends you don't know about?"

Mike stood up, scratched his head and was on the verge of a revelation, or so it appeared.

"Mike, what is it?"

"Viv, how about we go for a little walk?"

Mike shot a glance at Sally. She nodded reassuringly.

"Why can't you tell me here?"

David rose from his seat and announced, "I could step out of the room, if you would feel more comfortable?"

"David you're very sweet but there's no need for that. Sit down and have your tea," Sally smiled.

"Please Mike, anything you have to say to me can be said in front of David. He was a friend of Dad's too."

Mike lowered himself back into his seat and exchanged uneasy glances with his wife.

"What is it? I see something in your eyes."

"I honestly don't think I should tell you anything without consulting with your mother first."

"You know what my relationship with Mum is like. We weren't overly close when Dad was alive, just think how it's got to now."

"Oh Viv," Mike sighed, "I didn't realise how hard things were between you and your mother."

"We promised we'd make a visit this year and we will," Sally assured.

"What do you need to know Viv? I'm sure Joanna told you what happened."

"She told me about the accident. I know there's more to it, don't ask me to be rational, I just have a gut feeling that something's missing. For example, she told me my Dad had been fired, I don't know whether to believe it or not."

"As you know, your Dad loved America. The job allowed him to travel. In fact he was offered a relocation to be one of our American representatives. He wasn't fired. I think your Mum must have said what she said out of anger."

"That was the reason for all the arguments," Viv recalled her mother's hideous tantrums. Things were coming into perspective.

"I think so. Your Mum was dead against moving. She had a job, you were in school, she was right to worry. However, the constant arguments and fights took their toll on your father."

Viv nodded, assuring Mike that it was safe to go on.

"Your Dad met someone in America."

Somehow that information didn't ring true.

"What do you mean? Like a good friend?"

"A girlfriend, Viv."

If she felt her heart had been wounded previously, she was wrong.

"I've done the wrong thing by telling you this," he retreated and hovered by the open balcony. Sally promptly took his place.

"Honey, look at me, your father had never meant

anything to happen. Sometimes…"

"Things do." David finished Sally's sentence.

"That's right, David. Sometimes we can't control who we are going to meet."

"My Dad had a girlfriend?" she exclaimed.

Mike came back in, still flushed. Sally returned to her seat and Mike tried to finish what he had started.

"Your Dad was a good man. He loved both you and your mother. His lady friend had nothing to do with what happened."

"I think it has everything to do with what happened. Who was she?"

"I honestly don't know Viv. I really don't know."

"How long had it been going on for?"

"I don't know that either."

"Could you tell me just one thing and I won't ask you anything more on the subject?"

"Yes," he said solemnly.

"Was my Dad on his way to see her, the day he died?"

Mike looked over to his wife, Sally quivered and then put her face in her hands. Viv had discovered a whole new chapter in her father's life. She couldn't just step back and allow this information to wash over her. She knew where her journey lay and had to leave that instant.

◆

RENA HAD slipped back into her old routine like a fish in water. She enjoyed her Saturday morning trip round to the local shop where she would buy three newspapers and a carton of milk. It was a tradition Rena had no intention of changing. She was still intent on travelling and had to go over her itinerary that afternoon, but not before mid-morning tea and The Times.

As Rena strolled back into Willow Court she spotted her neighbour peering through her window. Rena had spied Joanna, they exchanged glances and she gave her neighbour a friendly wave. Joanna disappeared behind the curtains, only to open the door moments later. As Rena moved closer, she found her neighbour looking more tired than she had ever seen. Like her garden, Joanna was no longer in bloom.

"Hello Joanna, how are you?"

"Fine, come in then."

Rena wiped her shoes on the mat. The familiar unpleasant odour reminded her that Joanna still had a drinking problem. Rena held the door open to let in the morning breeze.

"I haven't tided up, forgive the mess."

The house was no cleaner than before, magazines and newspapers littered the kitchen. Empty cartons of milk had yet to be thrown out and an old curry container festered in the open microwave.

"Tea, Rena?"

"A cold drink would be fine. Joanna, is everything alright?"

She hadn't been herself in years but at this particular moment she looked drawn and old.

"No, not really. Orange juice did you say?"

"Sure. I'll have to get back to my Mum soon."

"Pull up a chair. No, not that one, I spilled tea on it earlier. Sit at the breakfast bar, we'll have our drinks there."

Rena obeyed.

"Are you home for the weekend?"

"No, I've decided that university wasn't for me after all."

"Ha!" Joanna livened.

"Excuse me?"

"I'm sorry Rena," she giggled nervously. "I just find it ironic that the cleverest girl I know has dropped out. It makes my daughter seem a hundred times better, so for that, I thank you." She sighed.

"That's not a nice thing to say."

"You know what Rena?" Joanna slammed the juice down and yanked a bottle of wine from the vegetable compartment. "Vivien doesn't give a damn about university. She couldn't just come out and say it, she had to lie to her own mother."

Rena watched as she failed miserably to light a cigarette.

"I've got the shakes. This is what alcohol does to you. May it never pass your pretty lips. Bloody cigarette," she scowled.

"Joanna, I can get my Mum over here if you like? You don't seem well."

"I'm fine, I always have been. You know that darling daughter of mine hasn't called once since she went on her little holiday?"

"You don't know where Viv is staying then?"

"No."

"I'm sorry Joanna."

"For all I know that man could be a rapist."

"David is a good man. He genuinely likes Viv. It's a good thing that she's gone away. The last year has been terrible for her," she paused and then was quick to add, "And you too. Maybe space is what you need. Anyway, it's so expensive to call from the States."

"I got fired yesterday Rena." Joanna's head dropped, tears filled her eyes.

"I'm sorry. I didn't know you were working."

"I was working as a receptionist. I turned up late yesterday morning. Just one morning, unfortunately I had a liquid breakfast, that didn't help matters in the slightest."

"I'll go and get my Mum. Maybe you'd feel better if you talk to her."

"Rena wait. She can't see me like this."

Rena looked at Joanna with such sorrow. A once beautiful and vibrant woman had been driven to such misery. Rena leaned over the breakfast bar and put her hand on Joanna's.

"Do you remember when you had a barbecue for Viv's tenth birthday?"

"What are you talking about?"

"It just popped into my head, that's all. You wore that pretty green dress. I arrived at the party with the exact same pink dress as Viv. She threw a tantrum and I started crying so you picked me up and took me into the garden and gave me a bowl of jelly."

"How do you remember that?" she smiled and pushed

the bottle out of reach.

"It was a happy time."

"I was quite attractive, back then, you know."

"You are now, Joanna."

"That was a long time ago," her expression hardened suddenly. "I just can't believe she hasn't called!"

"She will call. I'm sure she will be back soon. As soon as she finds what she wants she'll return and everything will go back to normal." Rena concluded, feeling that she'd assured Joanna quite adequately.

"What do you mean by, find what she wants?"

"I didn't mean anything by it."

"Rena, I know when someone is lying, that is something I know about. What did you mean by that?"

"Nothing at all."

"If my daughter is up to something, I have a right to know. If you're holding something back I'm going straight to your mother."

"Joanna, please sit down."

"Then tell me now," she demanded.

"Viv has gone to California because she feels there's more to her father's death. My mother told me."

"What's that supposed to mean?"

"She's gone to find out what happened to her father. The holiday was a pretext."

With one swift movement the wine bottle was hurled from the kitchen table and smashed against the wall. Rena braced herself for the fury that would ensue.

Within an hour of the revelation, David and Viv were

headed back to Los Angeles. She was unsure of her next move but she knew it would come to her eventually.

"So, do you think it's true?" Viv wavered nervously.

"It's a valid reason for your Dad's frequent trips," David replied gently.

"I need to find her, I need to know everything that happened."

"Affairs happen Viv, sometimes out of genuine love, sometimes out of boredom."

"How do you know?"

David shrugged nonchalantly.

"I'm hazarding a guess here but is that the reason you and your Dad fell out?"

"Maybe."

It was becoming clear that she had to be a lot smarter than this, if she was to figure out what he was hiding. David's personality was often as diverse as LA summers and British winters.

"David, isn't it time you made your peace with your Dad?"

David fiddled with the radio until a clear signal was found, luckily for him it was a loud song that seemed to drown out all potential conversation.

"I know where we're headed," she brightened.

"And where might that be?"

"City News, I need to speak to Guy Favor."


Joanna trod on what had once been a busy Lizzie patch. Rena was still inside the house trying to sweep up the shattered wine bottle, while Joanna strode to number eleven and hammered with her fists.

"Joanna, what on earth has happened?"

"I need to speak to you," she said desperately.

Carmen stepped back and Joanna made her way through to the lounge.

"Joanna where are your shoes? Look at you, you've cut your foot. I'll get the first aid kit. You stay right there."

Joanna sat shaking, and looked over anxiously as the door widened.

"Rena, where did you get to?"

"I cleared up the glass."

"I'm sorry if I frightened you."

Rena half-smiled but was reluctant to go any closer. Carmen hurried back and washed the cuts, before wrapping Joanna's foot with a thick bandage.

"What happened?"

"I got mad and smashed a bottle. It could have hit your daughter," she whimpered, putting her head in her hands.

"Rena, you were at Joanna's?"

"I went to have a drink with Joanna. I upset her."

"No," she interrupted, "You didn't, it's that daughter of mine always keeping things from me."

"What on earth happened?"

"I haven't heard from my daughter since she left."

"I'm sure she's just having a good time…"

"With a stranger! Now I've found out the reason why she is there."

"For a holiday Joanna," Carmen said gently. "She needs a break and by the look of it, my dear, you need one as well."

"It's my fault Mum. I told Joanna the main reason Viv wanted to go over there, she went to find out what happened to her Dad."

"Of course," Carmen said knowingly.

"How dare you?"

"I beg your pardon?"

Joanna snatched her hand back from Carmen's grasp.

"How dare you offer to help, when you've known all along why my daughter's over there. She's gone to meddle in things that will only cause her pain."

"Joanna, calm yourself."

"Viv has always confided in you," she spat. "You've pretended to be my friend when all you do is look down on me. The silly drunk woman from next door."

Carmen straightened and spoke quite firmly.

"That is not true. I have supported you and Viv as friends do. I have never spoken ill of you and never will. If Viv has ever confided in me it hasn't been to spite you. You know as well as I do, Viv can't move on in her life until she gets some answers."

"I've told her everything. Her father's death was an accident."

"I mean for herself, Joanna. Viv has to face it herself, she wants to find answers for her own peace of mind. Look, everything has got a bit out of hand. Why don't we have some tea, the kettle has already boiled."

"No, thank you," she replied quietly. "I've made a fool of myself."

"Don't be silly, and I insist on the tea. Rena did

you buy the milk?"

Joanna smiled apologetically, she had flown off the handle twice in the space of twenty minutes.

"I just don't understand why she couldn't tell me?"

Rena sat close while Carmen busied herself in the kitchen.

"I think there are some things you just can't tell your Mum."

"You're not like that with your Mum though?"

"You'd be surprised."

This brought some comfort to Joanna, she had always been secretly envious of the picture perfect relationship Carmen and her daughter shared.

"I behaved atrociously. I'm sorry if I scared you."

"Apology accepted. I think I know a way you might be able to speak to Viv."

"How?"

"Last night I was discussing my travelling plans with Mum. That is what I want to do for the next year."

"That's nice." Joanna brightened, though she didn't see where the point was going.

"I've just thought of it now. It might seem a little crazy. But seeing as though I want to start travelling and you're currently..."

"Unemployed?"

"The point is I want to go and see Viv in California. It would be my first stop anyhow. I've always wanted to go to the States. If you know where Viv is headed, we could go together? Even if we can't find Viv it would be a great break. Something different."

If Joanna had been eloquent at that moment, she would have been. Rena was the one little prayer that had been answered.

◆

THE SKYSCRAPER of City News looked taller than it had done before. The building rose high above the clouds. Viv wondered if the enormity before her was simply the manifestation of how big her problems had become.

"David, please come in. Just think how glad he would be to see you."

"Viv, he wouldn't. Trust me on this. Go and see Guy, that's fine."

"Will you pick me up?"

He began to chuckle to himself, "You sound like you're asking your parent if they'll be there to meet you after school."

"Very funny. Will you be here?" she pressed him.

"I'll be here. In an hour, prompt."

"Yes sir!" she mocked and watched him pull away at tremendous speed. He couldn't have got away faster.

It seemed as though the world had congregated on the twenty-third floor of City News. Rows of desks, private cubicles, people whizzing in and out as if every second counted and she figured in the world of reporting, it did.

"Who are you?"

"Oh, hello. I'm here to see Guy Favor."

"Oh yes? Did reception tell you to come up?"

"She did. Mary-Ellen rang Mr Favor a moment ago. He said it would be fine to come up."

"Hey Samantha!" Guy yelled over, "She's okay. She's with me."

Viv promptly made her way over; she was getting frostbite from standing too close to Samantha.

"Don't mind her. Uptight by nature. I think she's up for some kind of promotion in the next week. So, why are you back? Stalking me? After a date or something?"

"God no!"

"It was a joke," he replied, a little put out.

"Oh, sorry. I didn't mean it like that."

"Oh forget it. So, what do you want? You can sit by the way."

Viv paused and noticed that his attire was a little different from the other workers in the office.

"Are you going to talk? I haven't got all day."

"Why don't you wear a suit? I'm just wondering."

"I haven't worked at this god-damn paper for twelve years not to get a few privileges. I assume you're not here to quiz me over my dress sense?"

"No. Actually I came back for some advice. I did what you said, I went to see Mike Drake, the man you interviewed."

"And?"

"He knew something."

"What did he know?"

"My Dad had a…" she stuttered.

"Don't pause, don't stop, keep going, I've got a meeting in four minutes."

"He had a lady friend."

"That explains the frequent trips, I suppose."

"I guess," Viv sighed.

"Ignorance is bliss, huh? Don't worry about it, at least your Dad was happy."

"How do you know?"

"I don't, I'm just trying to make you feel better. Jesus! I don't get paid to talk to annoying kids all day, you're wasting my time here."

"I'm sorry, I'll get to the point."

"Finally."

"How do I find out who she is? Mike says he doesn't know her."

"That's easy. You need to go to the town where he was headed, Monterey right?"

"That's right."

"Ask questions. Do some research, look at what the local papers covered, go to the reporters, make yourself a nuisance, like you're doing now. Now scram, I got work to do."

The phone rang and Viv obligingly left Guy attached to his mouthpiece. She decided however that her time at City News wasn't quite over, as she made her way over to the elevator, the dark-suited Samantha was once again on her trail.

"Leaving so soon?"

"I was. But I was wondering if you could point me in the direction of Conrad Lancer."

"Mr Lancer is editor in chief, you can only see him by appointment."

"I understand, but it is quite important."

The elevator doors opened and a group of businessmen walked by, acknowledged Samantha, and then headed over to a large room at the far end of the office. Viv smelt the power and influence oozing from this gathering, and headed in their direction.

"Where do you think you're going?"

"Is Mr Lancer with those group of men?"

"I think I might call security. You've seen Guy, now I think your time here is up."

"This is important. I wouldn't dial that number if I were you."

Samantha smirked at her audacity.

"Big mistake," Viv went on, feeling a sense of superiority considering Conrad would be most disappointed if Samantha was the catalyst that jeopardised a reunion. "Samantha your promotion is in the balance, it could tip either way."

"I beg your pardon?"

"If you call security Mr Lancer won't receive an important message, and I think he will be most disappointed when he finds out who was the cause."

Samantha slammed the phone down, she was proud but not stupid, and she could not afford to take a chance, not now.

"It's the door at the end of the corridor."

Samantha marched off, job still intact though her ego was a little bruised.

Viv tapped lightly on the door.

"Come in."

She gripped the metal handle and peered across a corner office. A panoramic view of the downtown LA skyline extended before her.

"Hello, are you Conrad Lancer?"

"I am. Who might you be? Are you Brenda's new temp?"

"No, I've just been to see Mr Favor."

"Poor girl," he said in quaintly amusing tones, "Well come in then, sit down."

His warmth and humour cut through her preconceived idea of David's ogresome father. She wasn't even sure what she was expecting but she was pleasantly surprised.

"You didn't give me your name?"

"Viv Goddard."

"Name's vaguely familiar."

"Guy Favor covered my father's death."

"I'm very sorry Viv. I hope Mr Favor was nice to you out there?" His concern seemed genuine.

"Oh yes, he's a bit abrupt but I like him."

"Good, good. Now, what can I do for you?"

"I don't think I should even be doing this," she squirmed, as she sunk into her seat.

"Doing what?"

"I'm on holiday with your son."

The marker that he had been toying with, dropped onto the desk; Viv gave him a moment for it to sink in.

"My son is with you now? He's in the States?"

"He is."

Conrad leaned back in his chair and sighed deeply.

"This is quite a shock."

"I can imagine."

"Does he know you're here?"

"He thinks I'm here to see Guy Favor."

"I don't know where to begin!" he laughed nervously. "Are you seeing my son, Viv?"

"No, we're just friends."

"It's very considerate of you to make contact. I know this must have been your idea. As far as my son's concerned I don't even exist."

"I'm sorry," Viv said quietly.

"Don't be."

"I told him whatever your problems, it would be a good idea to make your peace. Or at least talk, if nothing else."

"And what did he say?"

Viv shook her head.

"Could you talk to him again, Viv?"

"What do you want me to do?"

"Invite him over to the house, tonight."

"I don't know if he'll listen. I'm betraying him even coming here."

"You're a good friend to do this. You must be close."

"I'll try my best. Where do you live?"

"If David agrees, he'll know. I'll also give you my number." He handed over a beautiful cream card with fancy gold font. "I don't care if you decide to turn up at three in the morning, I'll be there."

Viv turned to leave.

"Thank you Viv. Tell my son…"

"What?"

"Just…" he stuttered, "Tell him… nothing."

This time Viv felt regret sink in, if she did not deliver David, she might have broken an old man's heart.

After an afternoon of painstaking coaxing, David finally agreed to a reunion with his father, on the condition they would make an early appearance, and after dinner, an even speedier exit. It was now 5pm and they were headed directly into the heart of Los Angeles.

"So, where does you Dad live?"

"We're on Sunset now, he lives just off here."

"Do you mean, the posh area?"

"Beverly Hills to be exact, ma'am."

"Whatever he did, is it worth leaving this?"

Viv could not decide which side of the road to focus on first. The old theatres and novelty shops were a feast for the senses.

"Monroe! That woman looks like Marilyn Monroe. Will I see anyone famous?"

"Probably not. They'll be in the Hollywood Hills, behind their well-secured gates."

"This is exciting, it's so busy though."

"It's rush hour. Just enjoy the tourist scene now, we're headed north as from tonight."

"Why don't we park and then walk to his house, if it's just off Sunset?"

"This isn't a street in a town centre. It would take quite a while to walk to his house and nobody walks here."

Viv waved goodbye to the eclectic boulevard as they

headed up a long street that wound high into the hills.

"My goodness, he is a millionaire."

"So?" he replied defensively.

"I'm just observing. The prices in this area must be astronomical."

Every estate was gated, dripping with bougainvillaea and luscious greenery, making sure no passers-by could even glimpse the houses beyond.

"How long has your Dad been in this house?"

"Too long."

"So, you lived here too?"

"I did."

"Thought you were an east-coast boy?"

"I was, we lived in New York until I was ten, then we moved west. Shannen lived in the house next door."

"So, she's rich."

"Her parents are."

"What does Shannen do anyway?"

"She lives off her trust fund."

"Must be some trust fund."

They came to a halt, ahead of them a twelve-foot high wrought iron gate hinted at the luxury to come.

"Here we are."

"I think we've reached the pearly gates of heaven."

"More like the gateway to hell."

He casually leaned out of the window as if he were about to order fast food.

"David to see Conrad, please."

"Good evening Mr Lancer," the monotone voice droned.

"Sounds as though my Dad is treating the employees well."

"Very funny, just remember to be nice and give him a chance."

David proceeded at a gentle pace, the tree-lined drive opened up to reveal the most magnificent home Viv had ever seen. The huge white columns probably cost more than the collective houses that made up Willow Court.

"It's like the palaces I used to read about in fairy stories," she marvelled.

David pulled up on the gravel driveway and looked at the house he used to call home. Viv took the liberty of ringing the bell.

"I can see someone coming. Do you have a butler?"

David shrugged and took a few paces back.

"Good evening Miss Goddard, Mr Lancer."

"Good evening. My goodness what a lovely home."

"Phoney formality," David whispered, as they stepped into the reception area.

"Do come through, Mr Lancer is in the sitting room."

Viv didn't want to move a muscle; she wanted to absorb every inch of this startling opulence. From the grey marbled floor, to the magnificent orchid centrepiece. Seeing as they were missing the Disneyland experience, this house was the next best thing.

"Viv, how lovely to see you," Conrad put out his cigarette and made his way to Viv's side. "Thank you for coming."

Viv turned around to make way for David but he wasn't in the room.

"Is my son with you?"

"He was a minute ago. I think he's nervous," she whispered.

David did make his appearance and stood in the doorway, nonchalantly.

"David?"

David made brief eye contact but was more concerned with something he had seen on the floor.

"You must be thirsty. I'll get some cold drinks arranged while David can show you the garden."

Viv smiled, he was by far the sweetest millionaire she had ever met. Actually, he was the only millionaire she had ever met! He was strong and tall like David, but his demeanour seamed to deflate as he walked apologetically past his son.

"Well, that was rude. You could have at least acknowledged him."

"Come on, I'll show you the garden."

Viv had never worked so hard in her life. She was about to ask Conrad what the going rate was for holding a conversation single-handedly. Viv was thankful when he suggested a change of scenery; it gave her time to think about what her next topic would encompass.

"The garden is lovely Mr Lancer."

"Please call me Conrad."

He escorted her through the sun lounge, which led into the dining room where the table had been laid out for dinner. She marvelled at the beautifully embroidered napkins and decorative silverware. If only her mother could have seen her now.

"Is this for us?"

"Of course. It's not often I have my son over for dinner, accompanied by a lovely young lady."

Viv blushed as he pulled out her seat.

"Thank you."

She felt like a princess, she was living out a fairy tale, for tonight she was the Lady of the Manor and David was her grumpy husband – because some things just never change.

"Psst."

"I'm here for the food," he yawned.

"For a spiritual person, you're not being particularly forgiving to your fellow man."

The swing doors went back and forth as Conrad made his way to the head of the table.

"I'm afraid there's no starter. I hope steaks are acceptable?"

"My favourite." Viv was salivating over the thought of a meal, which didn't consist of cheesy puffs and ham rolls.

"The curtains are beautiful by the way, the whole room is gorgeous. So soft and snug."

"I had the drapes made especially, real Italian silk. The napkins are made out of silk too."

"I'm a bit clumsy, so I hope I don't spill anything."

"Don't worry, I'm the same."

"Thank goodness," she smiled coyly.

David muttered under his breath,

"Have you got something to say, David?" Conrad spoke up.

"No. Just admiring the Italian silk, Conrad," he replied dryly.

"Thank you. I wish you'd call me Dad, by the way."

Her salad remained untouched, wilted from the heat of the steak.

"I really enjoyed that."

"I hope you're not too full. There's cheesecake for dessert."

"I'm being spoilt."

"Well you're on holiday, you deserve to be spoilt."

David closed his cutlery together and sighed heavily.

"We'd better get going Viv."

"But we haven't had cheesecake yet."

"I'm full. I'll buy you one on the way."

"Hang on a moment. You've barely been here two hours. I have had enough of stepping around you like a baby. I'm glad you're here because there are things we need to sort out," Conrad said.

"I don't mind stepping out of the room. I think it would be good if you two spoke without me here," Viv volunteered.

"Thank you. You're welcome to look around the house. If you would like coffee Jeffrey will be around."

That was precisely the response she was hoping for, she was on tenterhooks to get up those stairs and she wasted no time in doing so.

"She's a lovely girl David. She's your girlfriend isn't she?"

"Viv's a friend."

"Very attractive, well-mannered, articulate. A definite improvement on Shannen."

"I don't want you talking about Viv."

"Very well. Was the steak alright?"

"We've had the small talk. I don't want to be here any longer than necessary. Let's just get this over with."

An attractive black haired woman stared out at Viv, her deep-set brown eyes were familiar. Viv took hold of the picture and spent a few moments wondering what she must have been like. David's mother was a truly beautiful woman. She carefully placed the picture as it had been before. It saddened her to think how disappointed Conrad would be to find out they would be leaving. The thought of what was being said downstairs made the hairs on the back of her neck stand on end, and she quickly made her way out of the room for fear of being watched.

"So where is the magnificent Anya?"

"The relationship ended six months ago."

"I'm going in ten minutes so I suggest you say whatever you want to now."

"Why the rush?"

"We didn't come to America especially to see you."

"Yes, I know. Viv mentioned what happened to her father. I presume she's here to pay her respects."

"Amongst other things."

"If you need help with anything. Money, accommodation?"

"We're fine."

"I heard from your aunt that you started your own business. How's that going?"

"Fine."

"I also heard – which really surprised me – that you're a man of the church now, and you have some special skill in that area?"

"Something you would never understand."

"Spiritualism is it? I'm not quite sure what that means."

"And you probably never will."

"What does Viv do then?"

"She's trying to discover that now."

Conrad paused, took a small sip of red wine and gently patted his forehead with the silk napkin.

"This isn't easy for me David."

"I don't know what you want from me?"

"I want my son in my life. Is that such a difficult thing to comprehend? I haven't seen you in three years. You just cut me out."

"I had every right to. Every reason to."

"I understand, if I could turn back time…"

"But you can't."

Conrad snatched at his glass and downed the wine in one.

"I've thought a lot about those last few months. You don't know the half of it."

"I remember my mother lonely, without the help or support of her husband."

"I remember something different. When I decided to divorce your mother I had no idea of the illness. I'd met another woman and fell in love. I'm not proud of it but it happened, and does happen. I expressed this to your mother and quite rightly she was furious. I let her know that her every need would be taken care of; she wouldn't want for anything."

David opened a can of beer, an attempt to quell his growing anger.

"I offered her the house. She told me she wanted something smaller," he quietened. "So I bought the bungalow. I told her to call if she needed anything. I was there if she needed me."

"You say you were there for her but all you did was throw money at her, you never once came to the house."

"I realise my absence was evident. When I found out your mother had cancer I called and called. I wrote her letters, all of which were redirected back to the house. She told me she didn't want to see me. I did try, David."

"You could have made the trip from your palace to the bungalow, you could have made an actual physical attempt to see Mom."

"I tried. I came many times when you weren't there. I knocked on the door, she blanked me every single time."

"That's not what she said."

"Your mother was angry."

"She had every right to be. The husband she was faithful to for twenty-seven years, suddenly decides he needs a younger woman."

"I didn't know of the illness when we separated, it was three months afterwards."

"Did you love Anya?"

"Very much. She was a good woman. A foreign

correspondent at the paper, a very intelligent woman."

"What happened to her?"

"Her work took her overseas."

"Wasn't that obvious?"

"I thought we could make it work, but long distance relationships are a disaster." Conrad paused and leaned in closer, "Your unwavering loyalty to your mother is commendable. I'm proud of you for the way you looked after her. I know she was proud of you too. When she did talk to me she would praise you as if you were a god, she called you her angel."

◆

DAVID HOLED himself up in his old room. After a considerable amount of wine and a great deal more beer, he thought it wise to stay the night. The maids kept the room spotless, as they always did when he lived there. It was like walking into a time capsule. As he surveyed his old map, there was a knocking at the door.

"David can we finish our conversation?"

"I've heard everything."

"Well, if you won't speak to me will you at least consider reading these letters?"

Conrad placed a pile of unopened letters onto David's bed.

"This is all the correspondence I wrote to your mother after she moved out. I begged her to let me stay in contact, to see her on occasion, pay medical bills, anything within my power. This should make you understand that I did try."

Conrad closed the door behind him and David was left to deal with an unopened past.

David was restless. It had turned one in the morning and he was still awake. He needed to talk to someone and tapped lightly on the guest bedroom door where Viv was sleeping.

"Viv?" he gently opened the door. She lay on her side facing the window. David lowered himself onto the end of the bed, hoping she might hear him. He had opened all thirteen letters and read them cover to cover.

"David, are you there?" she spoke loudly. "What time is it?"

"It's late. Don't shout," he whispered.

"What are you doing?"

"He gave me some letters that he wrote to my mother."

"What do they say?" she rubbed her eyes vigorously.

"Read one for yourself."

David went over to the wicker chair and gazed down at the grounds. Viv stretched out her hand, fumbling for the switch on the bedside table. Everywhere was so peaceful as she took in every word.

"David, if this isn't evidence enough to say that he cared for your mother then what is? He was really trying to get through to her."

"She never told me about the letters or the phone calls. It doesn't change anything though, he left her."

"For a legitimate reason. He left her because he fell in

love, not because of her illness. Can't you see that? I'm not defending him either," she was quick to add.

"What should I do?"

"I think you should make your peace, accept him back into your life."

"How?"

"Just tell him how you feel. How do you feel anyway?"

"Sorry for him more than anything."

"Well, that's something. Do you want to get in?" she offered.

"What?"

"You sound like you need a sleepover. I promise I won't pounce on you," she joked. David was glad; company was exactly what he needed. Once he lay beside her, Viv felt nervous for proposing it in the first place and rolled to the very edge of the bed, David had done exactly the same. There was room enough for two people in the space they had created, and yet she kept very still until sleep beckoned her once more.

◆

*"I saw you on the pier. You had a pretty bow in your hair. Why did you run away?"*

*The little girl in the yellow dress smiled and twirled around like a ballerina.*

*"I knew you'd come to America. I knew it!" she squealed, and jumped high into the air, spiralling into the clouds.*

*"Stop running from me!" Viv called out, but she had gone once again.*

"Stop running!" Viv was shaken violently from her dream.

"Viv it's alright, calm down."

She saw David's silhouette above her and pushed him away. She sat bolt upright, frozen.

"What's the matter?"

"I'm cold."

"You were dreaming."

The window had not been opened, but the wicker chair rocked to and fro to the beat of the nursery rhyme she could still hear playing in her head. She looked on, were her eyes deceiving her? Was the dream still playing tricks? It must be.

*I'm not running from you,'* the little girl said impishly, pulling a silly face.

Viv gathered the covers over her head.

"Do you see her David? Please say that you see her, on the wicker chair."

"She's letting me see her," he replied calmly.

Viv slowly emerged from the covers, clicked on the light and grasped David's arm.

"Don't be afraid, she's just playing."

The little girl poked out her little pink tongue and smiled sweetly, *'It's nice to meet you.'*

"Viv don't be frightened. Just say hello or she might go away. She wants you to hear her and wants you to reply."

"Hello little girl. I'm glad you've come to see me again."

*'I hope very much that you will come and play with me on my swing,'* she said in clipped little tones.

Viv pushed the covers aside and watched as she rocked back and forth, humming gently to herself.

"I would like that. Could you tell me where your swing is?"

*'You will know tomorrow. Goodnight pretty Viv.'*

Viv wanted to reach out and take her hand but as she leant forward the little girl was no longer visible. Viv kept very still and watched as the chair continued to rock back and forth.

"She's giving you clues Viv. Don't look so concerned, she'll be back. She wants you to know you're heading in the right direction."

"But the chair," she pointed, "is still moving."

"Because the little girl is still there. I'll let you into another little secret Viv; she's always with you."

The taxi pulled up outside Terminal 3 at 9am precisely. It was a wet and miserable day but the promise of warmer weather filled Rena with a sense of well-being.

"I need to get some sunglasses while we're here."

"I'll remind you, but I honestly don't understand why we're here so early? We don't fly until twelve," Joanna huffed.

"Joanna you should be excited, being at the airport is the best part of the holiday, don't you know?"

"Let's just say it's been a while since I've been on holiday."

Rena had promised herself to keep the luggage to a minimum, and was proud for bringing only one large rucksack. As they dragged their bags to an extended queue Rena felt she had to reiterate a concern.

"Joanna you mentioned that you knew where Viv would end up. How do you know that for certain without an address?"

"Rena, if my daughter's gone looking for answers. I know where she'll be."

"Has she called and given a contact number or an address?"

"I don't need an address."

"But how can we be certain?"

"We can't. I'm relying on my intuition."

"Okay, I'll trust you Joanna, I'm just so happy to be here."

Joanna watched the thrill of adventure painted on Rena's face. She made herself a promise that her aim for today would be to chill out, if only for Rena's sake.

Viv had launched herself into an early breakfast of pancakes, maple syrup, scrambled eggs and crispy bacon. Conrad cupped his coffee in both hands, smiling admiringly at Viv's enthusiasm for such a simple meal, that he took for granted as normal fare.

David had already left the table to put the luggage into the car boot.

"I think those letters have made him see your side of the story."

"I hope so."

"He'll just need time."

"I don't have much time, I'm getting old."

"You're not old Conrad. I'd better go and see if David

needs any help."

"Viv, I've got a few things that might come in useful. I hope you don't mind but I spoke to Guy Favor this morning and he gave me a brief outline of your plans."

"Not at all."

"Follow me." He led her into a dark study, it smelt of new leather and furniture polish. "Have this dictaphone and here is a list of good hotels in the area. I know you want to find out some facts about your father. The dictaphone might help you clarify your thoughts."

"I feel like a journalist. Thank you, that's very considerate."

"Will you come back?"

"It's really up to David. Can I ask how you left the conversation between you?"

"I told him I was always here if he needed anything. He said he appreciated the letters but it would take time for him to heal."

"Viv, are you ready?" she heard David call out.

"In a minute! Thank you for all the lovely meals and for letting us sleep over," she hugged Conrad, just as she would have hugged her father.

"You're most welcome Viv."

David turned and with a half-smile said, "See you soon, Dad."

"That's progress," Viv whispered quickly, and followed David out into the car. Conrad stood alone under his marbled portico and waved goodbye as the iron gates closed behind them.

They had stopped for petrol before heading out of Los Angeles; David had a long drive ahead of him.

"Are we there yet?" Viv whined.

"No, this is going to be a very long drive. We're going to leave the 101 at a town called San Luis Obispo. Route 1 takes us all along the coast to Monterey, it's simply stunning."

The day was bright and she was regretting not buying a pair of sunglasses.

"I'm going to miss your Dad's food. He must eat like a king."

"Well don't get used to it, miss."

"I won't," she sighed, looking out at the early morning traffic. "I wonder where these people are going, and whether they get visits from yellow clad little girls in the middle of the night?"

"People are visited all the time Viv. It's a fact."

She contemplated the word 'visited' and wondered if these visits were going to become more regular.

"That means she's not here to stay?"

"I don't know. You'll find out for yourself."

"How much longer will it take to get to Monterey?"

"A while, so don't be too eager. I'd save that inquisitive energy for when we get there."

It suddenly struck Viv that they would be passing the stretch of road where her father was killed and suddenly her excitable mood was dampened. She fell silent for the first time all morning.

"Do you want the radio on?"

"I don't mind," she replied absent-mindedly.

"Viv, I should have asked you about it yesterday, but are you feeling okay about what happened?"

"Do you mean us sleeping in the same bed?"

"No actually, but was that a problem?"

"No, it was fine. What were you going to say?"

"What happened at the party with Shannen. You haven't mentioned anything."

"I just hope she can sort herself out, and I hope she has called the police. That Tony was such a creep. I can't believe I ate one of his meat sandwiches."

David grimaced at the thought and replied, "As long as you're okay? You're the hero in all this. You followed your instincts, you knew the little girl was pointing in Shannen's direction. You did really well."

Viv extended her seat back and felt quietly at peace, knowing she had been of use. She let her hand slip by her side, almost immediately she felt the gentle touch of David's hand.

"So, how long will it take to get to Monterey?" she blushed.

"You already asked me that," he smiled.

◆

IT WAS mid-afternoon when David pulled into the car park that overlooked Monterey Bay. Viv had fallen asleep towards the end of the drive, and had been blissfully unaware of the stretch of road where the fatal accident occurred.

"We're here."

Viv poked her head from under David's leather jacket. A beautiful vista unfolded before her tired eyes. Boats moored in a pretty harbour, to her left, a long pier thronged with tourists.

"This is Monterey?"

"Beautiful isn't it? Come on, let's go for a walk."

Viv linked David's arm, laughing excitedly as they headed for the crowd. The boardwalk trinket shops bursting with nautical fare and the shrimp stalls, all vied for their attention.

"So, this is where my Dad loved to come."

They sat for an hour, people watching, to the music of cawing gulls. The breeze was gentle, it had a calmness she hadn't felt in the thriving hub of Los Angeles.

"Your Dad gave us a list of small hotels we could stay in. Do you want to go and have a look now?" David acknowledged her timing.

They left the small pier, still linked together, and headed on, once again.

The streets were busier than expected, they were bumper to bumper. The smell of the sea air, clicking cameras, fat ladies in over-stretched shorts and enormous T-shirts thrilled her senses. She loved Monterey too.

"I've just seen something which might get our plan underway. There's a church over there," David pointed.

"So?"

"Read the sign. Isn't it clear?"

"You're right, it says Spiritualist Church."

"I may be jumping to conclusions but it's pretty obvious that your Dad would have visited this church.

Make a note on your dicataphone. The church ought to be one of our first stops. Shall we check into a hotel first?"

Viv had a good feeling about the first name on the list. It was small hotel, a mere stone's throw away from the church.

"Afternoon ma'am, do you have two rooms for tonight?"

"No dear, just the one. It has two beds, would that be alright?"

"That's fine," Viv added.

"Do you come from Scotland? What a sweet voice you have."

"No, no, I'm English."

The receptionist was oblivious to the subtle differences of the English language, and continued with the things she knew about.

"Have you been to the aquarium, yet? I advise you to go there before you leave, it really is beautiful."

"Thank you. We'll do that."


The room was small but cosy. Chintz adorned every lampshade, wall and bedspread.

"The colours on these walls are the colours of my nightmares," David frowned.

"Oh don't moan, it's sweet. Is my accent really that confusing?"

He didn't reply but began to check out the bathroom.

"There's only room enough for half of me in here."

Viv pulled back the net curtains and looked down on the quaint street below. The view was picture perfect for a postcard.

"So, what do you think we should do first?"

"We need to find out why your Dad came here so much. The library should hold information on the Spiritualist Church, maybe he was a member. You also need to look up the local coverage of the accident, the journalists here might be able to shed some light."

"Can we go now?" she asked sweetly.

"Library, is it?"

"Afraid so, do you mind?"

"Not at all. I fly thousands of miles, drive all the way up the coast to one of the most scenic parts of California and you want to spend our time in a library. I couldn't think of anything else I'd rather do."

"Thank you."

Viv went in for a small peck on the cheek having gained a certain amount of confidence from the impromptu handholding. He smelt fresh and clean, he never wore a scent, he didn't need to.

"Let's grab a taco on the way." David knew he had a long afternoon ahead.


"Would you like a drink from the trolley?"

"A white wine."

"And you?"

"Ginger beer, please."

The flight attendant carefully placed the drinks onto their food trays with a smile.

"Look how small the bottles are. For an eleven and a half hour flight you'd think they'd be less stingy."

"Well, you're more dehydrated in a plane cabin. One glass is the equivalent of two I'm told."

"Cheers to that," Joanna grinned.

Rena wondered if Joanna's drinking would rear its ugly head time and time again, throughout the trip.

"Thanks Rena."

"For what?"

"Suggesting this trip. Inviting me along. I hope I'm not going to cramp your style too much?"

"I appreciate the company, after California I'll be on my own for a while."

"How long do you intend to travel?"

"Until the money runs out. I'm planning to head over to Chicago after California. I have friends in Illinois, well, my Mum's friends actually. They've offered me accommodation, so that's always handy."

"I think it's brave of you to decide to do this so quickly. Though I can't understand how the most academic girl I know has dropped out of school. I think it's admirable how quickly you've put your new plan into action."

This coming from Joanna, meant a lot, she never minced her words, "Thank you." she replied.

Rena looked out of the small cabin window at nothing but perfect blue sky.

"Where exactly do you think Viv will be headed? What does you gut instinct tell you Joanna?"

"Monterey."

The library would be open for one hour longer. Viv wasted no time in getting straight to the microfiche.

There was only one other person in the library, the assistant librarian who set up the system for her.

"If you need any further help, just let me know. I'm on front desk. My name is Richard."

David was having a drink outside, the driving had tired him out, and he was looking a little worse for wear. She promised herself that it would not take long and they would be able to get back to the hotel.

"January 2002," she murmured, hoping there would have been some decent coverage over the accident.

> *English businessman killed in fatal*
> *bike accident.'*

She was struck immediately that the content was scarcely different than that of the article Guy Favor had written. Still, she noted down the name of the reporter.

"I'll see you tomorrow, Marshall Williams," she planned.

"It's me again. Is everything all right? Looking for something particular?"

"Not really, just researching," she answered, trying to be as vague as possible. She felt awfully tired. The investigative journalist in her could not be roused at this particular moment.

"I could help you if you'd like? Tomorrow we're not open so you better make the most of it."

"I suppose I better then," she sighed and moved along so Richard could get a look in.

"How old are you?" he enquired a little unsure.

"I'm twenty-one."

"English aren't you?"

"I am."

"So, what are you looking for?"

"Articles on recent deaths."

"Excuse me?"

"Someone close to me died recently, a road accident. That's why I'm here."

"Oh, you poor thing, I know all about it."

"You do?" she said a little surprised.

"The whole town was devastated, still is. I pray all the time. In fact there's a service tonight I'm attending."

"You're probably mistaken, I wouldn't have thought the whole town would know."

"Of course, it was headline news. Are you family?"

"No. I'm sure we're talking of different people."

"I wondered if you were family because you have the same look as her. Thought you might be a cousin."

"I'm sorry but I don't know who you're talking about. My Dad was killed in a road accident a few miles from here, over a year ago."

"I'm sorry. I always open my big mouth."

"Who did you think I meant?"

"Isabel Sanchez of course."

"Who's Isabel Sanchez?"

"I'll show you if you'd like. Do you mind?" he moved closer.

"Of course not."

"The whole town was devastated. She was such a beautiful child. It happened four months ago. Her mother works part-time here."

The pages raced past in a blur, he then stopped and

enlarged a photograph.

"This is her. The photo was taken the day before she died."

Viv leant forward and stared at the monitor, total disbelief engulfed her entire being. It was as if a bad dream had spilled into reality, casting a shadow over everything she touched. She moved towards the screen and softly stroked the little girl's face. She wanted Isabel to jump from the black and white photo into colour. Viv knew the colours of her little yellow dress and her jet-black locks. She smiled right back at Viv.

"The picture has moved you miss, you look like you're crying."

"Isabel?"

"I'm sorry, I've done a terrible thing showing you this picture. Are you thinking of your father?"

"Could I just have a moment alone, please?" she asked quietly.

David had noticed the unusual activity and entered the library to investigate further.

"What's going on?"

"I'm so sorry, sir. I didn't mean to upset her. She told me a relative of hers had died. I assumed it was the little girl," Richard felt distressed by his clumsiness.

David looked closely at the screen.

> *'Isabel Sanchez, aged eight, was killed yesterday morning in a tragic car accident outside her home on Meadows Avenue...'*

David dropped his head in respect and removed Viv's hand from the screen. "Look at me Viv. We need to go outside and get some air."

"I don't get what it has to do with me?"

"We have to go now."

"This is all my fault, if there's anything I can do?" Richard ventured.

"There is," David said immediately, "Where do her parents live? Where is Meadows Avenue?"

"I'll show you on the map. Isabel's mother lives at number thirty-two, again my sincerest apologies."

"It's okay man, she just needs some air."

David held Viv's hand as they left the library, puzzled by what this all meant. She wiped her eyes and gulped down the last of David's water.

"Everything's murky. Everything I touch goes wrong."

"You're over-reacting, we need to get back to the hotel."

"No, we don't. I need to find Meadows Avenue."

"You're not ready. You haven't thought about what you're doing."

"I'm being followed by the girl in that picture."

"You're in no state to go now."

"She's trying to communicate with me, she wants me to know something. What do you think?"

"You're right, but I'm not letting you go there when you're this upset."

"Thanks," she replied coldly and drifted along until he caught her arm.

"It's important that you follow this through – I know that – but let's do it together."

Meadows Avenue was a community of people yet to recover from tragedy. The gardens had lost their colour. The roses looked limp and unfed.

"I feel uncomfortable just being here."

Viv stopped dead in her track. Her mouth dried as the sensation of panic gripped her body. She swallowed hard, anxious to produce the saliva to loosen her tongue. Flashes of her father laughing swept through her mind. Would all this effort and searching give her the closure she wanted so desperately? She would have high-tailed it back to the hotel if it weren't for his firm grip. At least David was predictable, never letting her get away with anything.

"We're here now. We may as well do this."

"I feel like I'm spitting sawdust. My breathing doesn't sound very good."

"It's just nerves. We're almost there."

House number thirty-two was partially hidden by a monkey puzzle tree. Viv was stumped by this eerie statue, beckoning passers-by to stop and take in its unusual form. The leaves, dark green, sharp and spiky looked lethal to anyone curious enough to touch, Viv wasn't. The house was small but perfectly formed. It had stared tragedy in the face but the stress lines had yet to show. She pushed the little white gate open and stood nervously on the porch steps. David peered through the window, making greasy fingerprints as he touched the sparkling glass.

"There's not much life in here. I don't think anyone's home."

One tap became three hard knocks in quick succession.

"I think you're right. Should we leave a note? No, that's a bad idea," she corrected her train of thought. "A face to face meeting is the only way to do it."

David met her disappointed gaze, "There was no guarantee anybody would be home."

"Are you sure no-one was in there?"

Viv peered through the window for her own reassurance. The room contained one green sofa and a small television set in the far corner. Viv hesitated to examine any one item in detail, it was already a gross intrusion of privacy.

"This seems weird. We'll come back later."

David frowned.

"Tomorrow then."

Her initial determination faded into dim hopelessness.

"We could camp out?" he joked.

"What if every time we come over she's out?"

She took one last glance and fixated on an object placed atop a small coffee table beside the sofa. She moved to the right of the window to get a closer look.

"What's caught your eye?"

"Probably nothing but do you see that hat on the table?"

"Yes, so?"

"That hat is familiar."

"Have you got one packed in your suitcase?" he joked and walked back towards the pavement, edging to get a move on.

"My Dad had a hat like that," she whispered.

"I asked my angels to guide you here and they did."

Viv swivelled round to hear who had made the admission. To her surprise a middle-aged woman, with an olive complexion, was standing by the garden gate. "My name is Rosa Sanchez. You're Vivien aren't you? I'm so glad to meet you."

◆

THE HALLWAY was filled with a profusion of orchids and lilies at every turn. It occurred to Viv to mention how lovely they were, but as she glanced up at Isabel's photograph, she realised what they all represented and decided to let the moment pass.

"Please come on through. Would you like tea?"

"Just a juice please, if that's okay," Viv smiled. David perched on the edge of a chair. Viv deliberately sat close to the hat, hoping that an opportunity would present itself and she could examine the object that had been taunting her from the moment she set eyes on it. Rosa appeared moments later with a tray of cakes and biscuits.

"You must be hungry. If you would like something more…"

Viv stopped her short, "This is very kind of you Mrs Sanchez."

"Please, call me Rosa."

She disappeared out of the room once again; David lunged quicker than Viv for the biscuit tray.

"Today feels like some obscure dream."

"Well prepare yourself because it's about to get stranger."

"What does that mean?" she frowned, but sat back as Rosa came back into the room, this time with a tray of liquid refreshments.

"I have orange and mango juice," she said nervously. She carefully placed the tray on the coffee table. Viv was halfway through her biscuit when she blurted out, "Where did you get this hat from?" It seemed a strange start to the conversation but it had to begin somewhere.

"It was a gift," Rosa smiled and sipped from her glass.

For some reason, it didn't feel appropriate to continue with this line of questioning.

"We were at the library earlier and I saw the article about your daughter, Isabel. I'm truly sorry. I wanted to come and meet you straightaway."

"Why was that?" she asked, still smiling gently.

"This is going to sound really stupid. I'm afraid to say because it might offend you."

"Please."

"Your daughter keeps appearing to me. I know that sounds ridiculous. I don't want to make you upset."

"You could never do that. I know she has been with you."

"It doesn't surprise you?"

"Please describe how you see her?"

"I see her like I see you now, as a person, though I always see her in the same yellow dress and the same yellow ribbon." Viv smiled as she thought of the little expressions she would make. "She teases me, you know, sticks out her tongue, runs away when I try to confront her, I suppose what any little girl would do. This sounds ridiculous. I feel embarrassed to even be saying it."

"Don't ever feel embarrassed."

"I think it's quite incredible how she led us here," David spoke up. "She appears at unusual moments, I think it's to let us know that we're on the right track."

Rosa smiled warmly.

"Don't you feel angry? When you're still mourning your daughter?"

"No, I think it's wonderful that my daughter is trying to contact you. She doesn't want to talk to me at the moment," she laughed, though it sounded strained.

"Why is she contacting me?" Viv said in all seriousness.

"Would you like another drink first?"

"Please explain it to me. You know something, you knew who I was the moment you saw me."

"This is going to be very hard."

"What is?"

"Explaining why it is that Isabel is with you."

"Just say it. Quick and painless," she added naively.

"Isabel wanted to meet you from the first moment she saw your picture."

"How would she know who I was? Were you a friend of my Dad's?"

Rosa stood, hesitated and then asked, "Would you like to step outside and take a breath of fresh air?"

"Please explain, I need to know."

Rosa sat back down.

"She is your sister but not how you imagine. She is not

a blood relation, but in Spirit you are. As soon as she saw you, that was it. In her eyes, you were her sister. You see, I met your father four years ago. As you know his job enabled him to travel and he so loved the scenery here. One day he walked into my church and we became great friends. Isabel was very young at the time and your Dad became, you might say, a father figure to her."

"Why didn't Dad tell me about this?"

"He was always going to. In the beginning he was worried you wouldn't understand, because in the beginning there was nothing to tell. We were friends for a long time but I soon grew to love your father. One day, Isabel was rummaging through his coat pockets, he always hid candy for her to find, and she came across your picture. As soon as she saw you she said, "There's my sister.""

"You and my Dad loved each other?"

"We did. I spoke to your father the night before he died. He was coming up to see us for the weekend. The last thing he said to me was that he couldn't wait any longer and that he had to tell you everything. He was planning on flying you over. Oh Viv, he loved you so much."

◆

VIV LOOKED down from the bay window. She was sat comfortably in the nook and fixed her gaze on a lonely street light. Viv took a bite out of the sandwich Rosa had made for her. David had decided to make use of the hotel bar; a nightcap to help him sleep easier. Events of the day had left both of their heads spinning. Viv glanced back at the bed where she had laid a large pink box. Rosa said it contained letters and pictures of Isabel and of her father, a memories box. She thought it best not to analyse its contents now. She needed to quieten her mind, and took peace in the tranquil scene outside her window. It was a quiet residential area, only the muffled laughter and soft candlelight of a family dinner disturbed the evening. It made her wonder what her mother might be doing this evening. Images of her falling down in a drunken stupor with no-one to help her; the thought made her heart race frantically. As she quietened again her gaze drifted from house to house, finally resting on the lonesome street light. Only now it illuminated a familiar figure.

"What are you doing?" she mouthed softly, tapping the window.

Without a second thought, she made her way down the narrow staircase and swiftly headed out of reception and into the cold night.

"Isabel! Wait for me."

Viv chased after her, twisting into unknown streets.

"I'm stopping. I don't know where you are leading me."

In front of her was a gated entrance to a small copse. A little oasis tucked away in the moonlit street. Isabel stood a foot away from Viv and smiled, beckoning her on.

"I can't go on for much longer. I'm tired Isabel. Can you hear me?"

Isabel stopped and looked as if she were going to speak.

*'I can always hear,'* she said softly, her voice locked in a whisper. *'We need to go in here,'* Isabel pleaded. Viv followed her through the foliage until they came to an enormous oak, its outstretched branch gently holding the swing Isabel had mentioned. She climbed on straight away and kicked off with her little black shoes. Viv made herself comfortable on a bench a few feet away. She was alone with Isabel but felt no fear.

"That's a nice swing. I used to have swing like that. But one day my Mum decided that she wanted a go and broke it."

Isabel smiled pleasantly but seemed to be more occupied with her swing.

*'You can have a go if you want?'* Her sweet sound was clearly audible this time, it wasn't a whisper, it was a real voice coming from what appeared to be a real little girl.

"I might break it. I'm much bigger than you."

Viv held her gaze this time, Isabel brightened, and for the first time she felt comfortable in her presence. She felt her eyes become heavy as the swing went back and forth, Isabel never tiring, not even for a moment.

"Isabel? I went to see your mother today. Do you know that?" she ventured.

*'Yes, I do.'*

"Isabel, you'll fall and hurt yourself. You're swinging too high."

Isabel's face exploded into a fit of girlish giggles, Viv half wanted to join in, then realised the impossibility of the comment she had just made.

*'My Mummy likes you very much.'*

"I like her too Isabel. You know, my favourite colour is yellow. I wish I had a dress like yours."

Isabel stopped swinging, jumped off and as she came closer she raised her little face and smiled. Viv was taken aback as Isabel looked on adoringly, she didn't warrant such praise but it was all in a look. She turned and skipped playfully back to the swing, jumped on the seat, grasped the ropes and kicked off once more.

"You really like that swing Isabel. Did you help make it?"

With every question Isabel swung higher, so high she could have touched the clouds with the tips of her patent leather shoes.

"It's cold Isabel. I think I'd better go now."

Isabel dragged her shoes on the ground to slow herself but no sound could be heard.

*'Daddy wants you to look at the pictures,'* and at that she vanished from Viv's presence. Viv was alone in the wood. The swing started to rock back and forth and began to pick up speed again. Isabel was nowhere in sight.

"Isabel, are you still there? I have to go now." Viv smiled a smile of confidence and headed for the comfort of the street lights.

By the time she returned to the hotel room, David was already lying on his bed. "Where did you go?" he yawned.

"Had a date with Isabel."

"At this time of night?" he sighed wearily and closed his eyes. "She really cares about you." The day's events had finally caught up with him. Viv moved closer and put her face next to his. She would leave it to fate to decide the consequences and pressed her lips softly against his. David's eyes flickered open and she pulled away quickly, only to be stopped by a strong hand which stroked the back of her neck and pulled her in closer. She had one regret at that moment, that she hadn't kissed him sooner.

◆

THE FOLLOWING morning proved to be just as beautiful as the day before. David took Viv's hand as they walked along Meadows Avenue. They shared an awkward silence for an eternal thirty seconds. Viv was quick to rectify the lull.

"Where do people commute to?"

"Silicon Valley, I suppose," he suggested, rather than confirmed. Commuters didn't interest him. He tugged her hand and as she turned he took Viv's blushing face in his hands.

"You don't regret anything?"

"Nope," she smiled coyly.

"Are you sure?"

"David we kissed. We haven't slept together, yet."

"Yet?" he smiled.

Viv pulled away, embarrassed.

"I think we better get to Rosa's."

As soon as Rosa greeted her special guests, she ushered Viv upstairs to show her what Isabel had always wanted her to see. Isabel's room was the prettiest she had ever seen. Viv touched the little pink pony whose tail had been painted yellow.

"She loved colouring in. Unfortunately that included most of her toys."

"Yellow was her favourite colour I'm guessing?"

"It sure was. I would try and make her wear different colours but she was very clear that yellow was her colour of choice."

"Isabel took me to a little wooded area last night. There was a child's swing."

"The swing your father made for her."

"She told me that my Dad wanted me to see pictures. Pictures of what?"

"Everything your father wanted you to see is in the pink box I gave you."

Viv's attention returned to the room, it was immaculate. A small vanity unit brandished little bottles of pale pink nail polish and small bejewelled hair clips. Her bed was draped with a white lace throw covered in small yellow ribbons. Above the headboard were pictures of horses and dolphins and of herself.

"My Dad took that picture!" she shrieked. "I remember Dad taking that picture before one of his trips. He told me he wanted a picture of me to show his friends."

"It was to show Isabel. It was her favourite picture. She loved your long dark locks. You are sisters in looks also."

Viv felt her heart leap when the inevitable question could no longer be suppressed.

"Rosa, what happened to Isabel? How did she die?"

Rosa answered, unflinching,

"My baby was playing in the garden, spraying the

flowers with the garden hose. I told her not to, we had just been to church and she was wearing her best dress, I didn't want her to get it ruined. She didn't like me telling her to stop and refused to come inside. I remember going back into the house as the phone had started ringing. She must have opened the gate at that moment. She loved to hide behind the trees and jump out at the neighbours to make them laugh. This time it wasn't a neighbour."

David was still in the kitchen when he heard their footsteps on the staircase. Rosa wiped her eyes and sat down on the sofa and kept a firm hold of Viv's hand. She seemed unwilling to let it go.

"I think I know what Isabel wants me to do."

"What would that be?" Rosa dried her eyes.

"She just wants me to say goodbye."

"Goodbye?"

"Yes, my Dad also. She's wanted me to acknowledge her all along, I just didn't know it then. This evening in the copse, at sunset, I want us all to say goodbye."

"That sounds perfect," Rosa replied proudly. "So, is that what you and David got up to last night. Planning this?"

With a glint in her eye, she replied, "Amongst other things."

Rena felt the car jolt, then all was calm. Her left arm was being shaken. She tried in vain to ignore it but the shrill pitch reverberating throughout the car, made her come to.

"We're here! Wake up and look at this view."

Rena had been overloaded with beautiful scenery for most of the journey. It felt comforting to know that they had finally come to a standstill, after what seemed like an interminable amount of time to be in a car.

"We're here," Joanna enthused. "I can't wait for my bed, I'm exhausted," she exhaled deeply, as she wound down her window to smoke.

"It is beautiful, my Mum visited the west coast a long time ago with my Dad. Have you been here before? You knew the way without the map."

"Once, about ten years ago. I was on holiday with Simon."

"So, Viv has been before, is that why you knew she'd come here?"

"Viv hasn't been here before. She stayed with Simon's parents while we were away."

"Oh look! Do you fancy a walk over to the pier?"

"Shall we check into a hotel first?"

Rena nodded politely, though she was dying to stretch her legs.

"As soon as we've found some accommodation, we'll look around the town."

Joanna flicked the remainder of her cigarette out of the window and started the car. They were, once again, on the move.


"I want our private service to be colour co-ordinated. Yellow flowers would be the most appropriate."

"Maybe you should consider a career in wedding planning?" David joked.

"Ha, ha, funny man. Seriously, I just want to make an effort. Do you think…" Viv's face darkened suddenly, "Do you think this is a stupid idea?"

"Viv this isn't for anybody else, it's for you. You need closure on this thing. Rosa needs it too. The flowers sound wonderful. Just think of it as a way to say goodbye to the person you love."

Viv lifted the roses to her face. The fragrance was divine.

"People I love," Viv corrected.

Viv placed the flowers on the counter, "I've decided on the yellow roses."

## Later that Afternoon …

"Viv, you've been in there for an hour. We have to leave for Rosa's."

"I'll be out in a minute."

David had managed to retrieve a jacket, which lay at the bottom of his rucksack. He had packed it, just incase. This evening seemed an entirely appropriate event to get spruced up for. Viv appeared moments later to David's surprise.

"You look incredible."

"You too," she blushed. "You clean up well, your jacket is very fetching."

Viv smoothed down her black locks and caught sight of herself in the dressing mirror. Her pale pink dress fitted her even better than before. She made a mental note that stress levels assisted in shedding those few extra pounds!

"I like what you've done with your eyes by the way."

"It's just mascara."

"Well you look great."

"Thank you David."

"You don't need to thank me."

"I mean thank you for everything. I wouldn't be here without you."


"The Rose Hotel, that will do. Let's get the bags out."

"Joanna should we check that they have vacancies first? All the other hotels we've tried were full."

"They'll have rooms."

A limp cigarette dangled from her dry mouth as they lugged their suitcases up the steps to reception. Joanna hit the bell with force, and an elderly gentleman popped his head around the corner.

"Ma'am, there's no smoking in here."

"Sir, have mercy on me. I've been driving for hours. Have mercy," she whimpered.

Her dramatics brought a smile to the gentleman's face.

"You finish that one, it's okay to smoke in the bar."

"You're a true gentleman. The last of a dying breed I'm sorry to say."

"How can I help?"

"Do you have two rooms for the night?"

"We do ma'am."

Joanna handed over her credit card.

"Joanna do you need some money?"

"This one's on me; for putting up with my drinking and smoking."

"You're from England."

"How did you guess?"

"We have two other British guests staying with us at present. A very charming couple. The Brits seem to enjoy coming here."

Joanna turned to Rena, "Sweetheart, do me a favour and put this cigarette out for me."

When Rena was out of earshot Joanna leaned over the desk, "You wouldn't by any chance be able to tell me who they are?"

"I can't give names, I'm sorry."

"Could you describe them? Only I have friends travelling up the coast, you never know it could be them," she laughed.

"Well, they looked nice earlier. The young lady was in a pink dress, the gentleman very smart. He's a little older than she is. Does that sound like them?"

"Possibly," Joanna wondered, as she remembered the pink dress she had brought Viv for her twenty-first birthday.

"Ma'am are you alright?"

"Never better," she smiled.


Viv scattered yellow roses under the tree and placed a bouquet on the little wooden swing.

"This is so lovely, the flowers are beautiful, Viv. Thank you so much," tears formed in Rosa's eyes.

"I'm glad you like them. I haven't prepared a speech though, and I'm an appalling public speaker."

"You're with friends Viv."

Viv took hold of the frayed rope and wondered if Isabel might be watching over.

"I came here last night. It was so lovely to talk to Isabel, I can't believe I have such a beautiful sister."

Viv listened to the leaves crumple underneath David's heavy shoes. He moved closer beside her. His eyes flickered and he seemed to lean on Viv for support.

"David are you alright? What's happening?"

"I need you to sit on the swing."

"It's Isabel's swing and I'll almost certainly break it."

"Please."

His manner broke the serenity of the moment. Rosa stepped forward out of the shadow and watched intently. Viv couldn't help but kick off the ground. She hadn't been on a swing in years. David stayed stationary and looked straight at her.

"Spirit wants to contact you."

She dug her heel in the grass and came to an abrupt halt.

"Do you mean Isabel?"

"Your father, he wants to speak to you."

From behind, Viv heard a gentle and loving sigh from Rosa.

"Can I see him?"

"I don't know if he can let you. I can hear him Viv. Would you like to speak to your father?"

"I don't know what to say." She ought to have been thrilled, but the unknown had clouded her judgement. What if her Dad was disappointed in how she had behaved over the past year?

"Yes, of course I want to speak to my Dad."

This was what she had dreamed of for the past year, that God would bring back her father. Today, her prayer had been answered.

David breathed in deeply and then exhaled very slowly. Viv was on tenterhooks.

"Your father is passing on his love from Spirit," David closed his eyes once more. The timbre of his voice becoming lighter and softer.

*'Sweet daughter, words cannot express the admiration I hold for you. Your kindness and consideration for all people is a joy to watch. I congratulate your strength over the last year. A year that has been the most difficult of your life. As a father, I could not have been prouder. You have been a pillar of strength for your mother and you could not have done better. Your mother is also so proud and loves you dearly, though she may not always show it. Your life is at an exciting stage where anything is possible. You have a bright future ahead. Your strength of character and sensitivity are your greatest tools which you must use to help others.'*

"What is my path, Dad?" she spoke up.

*'Vivien, your enormous spiritual gift must be nurtured. It will grow stronger over the years. Your relationship with Isabel will grow, and she will be able to guide you when you feel your path is clouded. She too is enormously proud. I have one thing to ask of you while you are here. A young woman needs your help right now. I have been watching over her but I feel she needs the help of a like-minded young woman, who she can relate to. You were meant to come here for many reasons and one of those is to help this woman. At midday tomorrow she will be attending*

*church. She has suffered great tragedy and needs your help. Tomorrow you will give her a reading. That is your objective while you are here.'*

"Wait! I'm not a Medium. David's the Medium, he can channel."

David shook his head violently as if he were battling with a thousand voices inside his head.

"Rosa what's happening?"

Up until that moment Rosa had remained silent, she now felt it was her time to speak.

"Sweetheart, David may have other Spirits who wish to communicate. He is in no pain. He is in trance. If you have any more questions, ask now."

"Dad, I don't even know her name."

*'You don't need to. I will contact you. Goodnight my child and God bless.'*

◆

Viv ALLOWED the lapping waves to rush at her feet. The hazy pink backdrop cast a gentle glow over the expansive big blue. Viv decided the best time to visit the beach was at sunset.

"I'm back," David called over. "One fish taco, one burrito and two Buds. A veritable feast. What a picnic!" he joked and laid the food out onto his jacket.

"Strange time to have a picnic!" Viv called out and joined him moments later, digging her feet well into the sand. "David isn't this the craziest trip?"

"It seems that way."

"I can't believe my Dad wants me to do a reading tomorrow," shaking her head in disbelief.

"You can do it. Trust your Dad, all you need to do is free your mind and Spirit will do the rest."

"David, can I ask you something?"

"Ask whatever you want."

"Do you think you will see your Dad again?"

"I know I'll see him again and when we do meet, hopefully, we'll have a better understanding. Just at this moment is not the right time. I want you to feel comfortable about tomorrow, that's the most important thing we have to concentrate on."

Viv sank her teeth into the soft taco.

"So, how do I channel? What kind of 'state' do I have to be in?"

David leaned in and placed a salty hand over her eyes, an indication they should remain closed.

"It isn't necessary to close your eyes but you might find it easier this way. If you can, empty your mind, or envisage the colour green which is naturally calming."

"Then what do I do?"

"Take a deep breath and ask Spirit to visit you. What you must remember is that your Dad has assured you he will be present tomorrow. He will come to you."

Viv flicked the specks of sand from her face and gazed at the ocean before her.

"I know he will. I just don't want to make a complete fool of myself. Do you ever get nervous before you give a reading?"

"All the time, because it isn't really me who is giving the reading, is it? Therefore I don't know what I'm going to say. We better get back to the hotel," he stood up, wiping the sand from his blue jeans.

"We haven't finished eating yet."

"We'll pack up the food and eat it back in the room."

"Why? It's only early."

"Your mother has just arrived."

In the darkened hallway Viv watched as a familiar figure walked towards her. Silhouetted by the lamp at the end of the hall was her mother, exactly how David had said.

"I can't believe you're here," Viv moved closer and hugged her mother. "This is incredible. Let's go inside and talk, there's so much to say."

As Viv jiggled the key in the door, Joanna wrapped her arms around her daughter and breathed a sigh of relief.

"I'm so glad I found you sweetie. I was angry that you didn't call but I'm just so happy to see you."

"That's another thing," Viv broke away momentarily as she opened the door. "How on earth did you find me?"

"Call it a mother's intuition or maybe I know what you have come looking for."

Joanna placed her hand on top of her daughter's and sank into the springy bed. She turned to her daughter, "Rena is with me too, I told her I needed to speak to you alone."

"Rena's here! This is too bizarre."

"So, where is this David character?"

"He went to the bar."

"That doesn't surprise me at all," she tittered sarcastically.

"Mum, why are you here?"

"I know what you have come looking for. Have you found out why your father was here?"

"Yes Mum. I know about Rosa and Isabel," she replied quietly.

Joanna pursed her lips tightly and immediately started to light up.

"Mum, this must have been so hard on you, but I'm glad I found out, I had to. That explains why you and Dad couldn't get along. If only you'd told me sooner, you wouldn't have had to carry this burden around on your own."

"You were never meant to find out, that was my job to never let you find out."

"Don't be upset. You can relax now, there's no need to be worried any more, no need for secrets, no more lies."

Joanna turned sharply to her daughter and took hold of her hand, "Please tell me you're coming home. You must come home."

"Of course I will. Not yet though. There is something I have to do. In fact, I would like you to come with me to the local Spiritualist Church tomorrow at midday. There is something I want to show you."

Joanna let go of her hand.

"When will this end Vivien? Spiritualist Church? I'm guessing that woman will be there tomorrow. I won't go Vivien."

"Please Mum, there is something you have to see. It might make you understand why I'm so interested in Spiritualism. Just think about it, now try and get some rest."

Joanna touched her daughter's face and left the room. It seemed now that every important person in her life had congregated in this one town. If there was such a thing as synchronicity, it had manifested itself in the seaside town of Monterey that night.

◆

VIV EYED up the formidable stage she would be gracing in thirty minutes. The prospect overwhelmed her.

"Look how many seats there are. Do you think they will all be filled?"

"They'll be filled," Rosa replied confidently, already making herself useful, placing comfortable cushions onto the hard wooden seats.

"Rosa, what happens if I don't hear Dad's voice?"

"Your father will not let you down. Your task is to give some young lady a reading, no-one else."

"I'm going back stage, I don't feel very well."

"A classic case of nerves, nothing more."

"I would probably feel more comfortable if I had a drink down me!" she moaned and trailed off to the back of the church. David was already in conversation with one of the Mediums sharing the stage with Viv that afternoon.

"Viv, I would like you to meet Pauletta, she will be leading this afternoon's service."

"Nice to meet you, Pauletta. I hope I don't embarrass you up on stage. My Dad is to blame if I draw a blank," she half-joked.

"Viv, you have nothing to be nervous about. We're a nice bunch, I promise."

Pauletta had a warm and comforting smile, she reminded Viv of Rosa albeit with longer hair and a good few inches taller.

"Just to let everyone know," Rosa interjected. "People are coming through the doors. Good luck sweetheart, I'll be watching."

Viv had visited the rest room four times in the space of fifteen minutes. As she took her place on stage, next to Pauletta, she wished she had visited a fifth time. She looked down at the table afraid to watch the growing congregation. She searched her peripheral vision and found David and Rosa taking their seats to the side of the stage. The only people left to arrive were her mother and Rena.

"This afternoon we will be hearing from a guest speaker who has flown all the way from Great Britain. This is Miss Goddard's very first service, so please wish her well. Thank you."

A welcoming round of applause ensued. Viv levelled the microphone and began,

"Good afternoon ladies and gentleman. As Pauletta said, I'm very new to this, so do forgive me if I'm a little shaky. I might not be as accurate as the more experienced Mediums, but I'll have a go anyway," she smiled, surprised that public speaking was not as frightening as she expected. As she looked down on the eighty strong congregation two late guests stood still at the back. She smiled nervously at her mother and Rena. The inevitable nerves kicked in.

"I'll start then," Viv hesitated, remembering to close her eyes, and tried as hard as she could to relax. She erased all images of her expectant audience to focus her mind purely on her Dad. A low hum began to circulate around the room. Voices desperately trying to get her attention. Momentarily she opened her eyes, surveyed the crowd, though nobody had said a word. Viv closed her eyes once more. The talking had now become audible. It wasn't a sound of ordinary people, but as she stilled her mind her Dad's voice came through.

"I would like to come to the young lady, third row, in the black jumper."

Viv knew instantly that the fragile looking blonde girl was the person her Dad had wanted her to help.

"Me?"

"Yes miss, would it be alright if I pass on a message from Spirit?"

"Of course," with an apologetic manner she lowered her gaze and asked, "May I ask who is with you?"

"Yes, my own father wants to pass on a message to you. Could I also have your name?"

"It's Lorna."

Griping the microphone with clammy palms, she passed on his message word for word. It seemed as though many Spirits were still vying in the background to get their messages across, but her resolve stayed firmly with her father.

*'You must not leave, Lorna. Thoughts of running away have been racing through your mind in the last four months, have they not?'*

"Yes."

*'The death of a loved one is a heavy burden to bare. Though you want to hide away, a young boy needs your guidance, your love and companionship. This is your younger brother is it not?'*

"Yes."

*'He looks up to you now and believes in you, just as your father did. You are not alone Lorna.'*

"Thank you."

*'Your father was your main supporter, was he not?'*

"Yes," she swallowed hard.

*'This person believed in everything you did. Even now, he watches down on you. Your father is very proud. Do not give up on all you set out to do. Remember your career chart, you and your father would talk for hours about all your plans, please do not forget. It is so easy to choose the wrong path. It is time to move out of the dark and into the light. It is time.'*

"Thank you!" Lorna shouted, oblivious to the crowd around her.

Viv kept her eyes tightly shut throughout the reading, conscious of the disapproving looks from her mother. By blocking out the audience, she had achieved total concentration. Lorna's intervention broke her train of thought and she could no longer hear her father's voice.

"I don't know anything about your life Lorna, I'm just repeating my Dad's words. I hope they have offered you a source of comfort."

"They have, though I can't help missing my Dad." Lorna leant on the comforting shoulder of a relative in mourning.

"I know."

"I'm grateful for everything you have said."

Lorna's inner strength showed through as she spoke.

"I miss my Dad very much too, but if I helped you in any way Lorna, then I'm happy for you."

Viv took her leave of the stage, surprised to receive a standing ovation. The piercing wolf-whistle was distinctly David's. Forget spiritual congregation she thought, these people were rockers. A nervous smile spread across Viv's pink cheeks as she stole her last glance at Lorna before disappearing behind the curtain.

◆

Viv knew that shiny black hair anywhere. It was still a mystery how her friend had managed to fit in a trip to California. Rena was already deep in conversation with an older gentleman from the congregation, when Viv decided to make a friendly intervention.

"Excuse me but shouldn't you be in lectures?"

Rena whipped round and lunged at her friend.

"Well, nice to see you too," Viv laughed, it was wonderful to see her best friend again.

"Viv! I can't believe you. You're a Medium!"

"A fledgling more like. Rena, you're in America! What happened?"

"I finished university. It wasn't for me, simple as that."

"Just like that?"

"I need more time to think about what I actually want to do. Plus, this gives me the perfect opportunity to see what you've been getting up to. A lot it appears." Rena stepped back. She was looking at a new woman in every sense. Viv was glowing with confidence, shrouded in a new light Rena hadn't seen before.

"I found out so much about my Dad and his life out here. There's so much to say, I don't know where to start."

"It can wait for another time, I know your Mum is waiting for you outside."

"Where are you headed next? Home?"

"Not quite yet. Chicago is my next stop, but I'll hang around here for a while."

"Thank you so much for coming to see me. It's really touching."

"You've done so well. My Mum would be proud of you. Just wait till I tell her about this."

Joanna stood a little way from the church but close enough that her daughter could see her. She watched tentatively as Viv appeared on the church steps with Rena, and the young woman she had chosen from the congregation. Viv and Lorna hugged with genuine affection, until Viv's attention wandered over to the blossom tree where her mother was waiting patiently. Viv said her goodbyes and moved towards her, hopeful that she would be pleased.

"Mum, do you want to go somewhere and chat? We could sit on the bench over there?"

Joanna was expressionless. Viv looked for any sign that she was pleased with what she had heard in church, but Joanna kept her cards well hidden and revealed nothing.

"I know what I said on stage must have sounded so alien to you."

"Actually, I was quite surprised. You clearly have a gift in that area." Joanna swallowed hard.

"So you believe?"

"Vivien, I'm not sure what I believe. That young woman could have been an actress, a friend or she could be genuine. But, if what you said was true, then you do have a gift."

"So do you Mum, the gift of foresight if you ask me. I still don't know how you knew I would be here, but I'm glad you are anyway. Life is going to get better for us from now on. I think we've turned a corner."

"How do you mean?" Joanna wondered.

"We don't have to lie to each other any more. You don't have anything to hide and neither do I."

"Will you come home with me?"

"I will come home Mum, when I'm ready. Please don't wait for me. I'm not out here to spite you or to make you unhappy. You have to understand that I'm an adult now."

Joanna had exercised perfect restraint thus far, though all she really wanted to do was take her beloved daughter home.

"I miss you so much, Vivien."

"I know you do." Just as Viv was beginning to feel guilty

for disappointing her mother, she reached into her pocket for a photo she had recovered from the pink box.

"You'll never guess what I found yesterday. Rosa gave me a box Dad made up for me; it's filled with silly notes and pictures. Look what is written on the back."

> *'To my darling daughter, love and*
> *happiness to you always, Dad.'*

Joanna took a bewildered glance at the picture. "It was taken when your father and I first got married. I don't know why he kept this picture."

"Don't you know?" Viv asked surprised.

"No, I don't," Joanna sighed deeply.

"Because you were in love. It's a lovely picture. Dad wanted me to have the picture so that I would never forget. No matter how things turned out, that what you once had was real."

"I appreciate the thought, darling. While we're on the subject of exchanging memorabilia, I thought you better have this."

"John Wayne! You travelled thousands of miles with John Wayne in a carrier bag?"

"Well, he was always your good luck charm. I couldn't throw him away. Maybe this might remind you of the good times we used to have. Maybe this will prompt you to come home."

Viv was genuinely touched by her mother's gesture, though she wasn't quite sure the cassette would work in an American VCR.

"Dad used to tell me stories which, I know now, stemmed from his spiritual beliefs. He told me about these people called silent heroes. Angels who surround us all the time and for most people they never know that they are there. Dad said I had guides and when I was old enough to understand I should find out more about these heroes."

"So who are your guides Viv?" she enquired sceptically.

"My Dad for one. I know he is with you also Mum and cares about you very much. I also have another very special guide who has been with me for years and I didn't even know it."

"And who is that?"

"You of course! Sure you don't come with a pair of attachable wings but you've always been there for me Mum. You don't have to be scared any more."

Viv had that same feeling of unimaginable happiness she used to experience as a young girl on Christmas morning. She had followed through her father's wish and had managed to assure her mother that life was going to be better for the both of them. There was only one piece of the jigsaw missing. As she darted up the stairs of the Rose Hotel, she realised the piece was David.

"You'll never believe what just happened..." Viv bellowed, cruelly cut short by the sight before her. "You're packing?"

David's rucksack was unzipped, clothes spilling over the top. They hadn't even been folded; he was clearly in a rush.

"What's going on?"

"Don't sound so down. Carry on with what you were saying, you sounded so happy."

"I was," she replied, totally deflated after her initial effort.

"You have every reason to be happy," he walked over and took her face in his warm hands. "You're a fantastic Medium and that was your first show – so to speak."

"You still haven't answered my question."

As David let her face go she felt her chin drop, her whole body felt heavy and she cleared a space on the bed to sit.

"I have to go Viv."

"Do you mean we?" she stressed.

"You've done amazing. You've followed through on everything you set out to do. I'm not much use to you any more."

"How could you say that? I wouldn't be here if it weren't for you. I don't understand why you're in such a rush to leave? We can finally have a holiday."

"I can't Viv."

David was resolute. Viv was finding it hard to fight back the tears, and was swallowing harder than she ever had before.

"So, what are you going to do now? Go back to England?"

"Not yet, unfinished business to sort out. Anyway, you need some time for yourself. Think about what you want to do next. It won't be much fun for you, following me around."

"It will. Listen to me, just don't go yet. I have someone

I need to say goodbye to first. Promise you won't go without me."

David paused, and chucked the final shirt on top of his rucksack.

"I won't go without seeing you first."

Viv couldn't wait to get out of the room. She raced downstairs with the same energy as when she had climbed up only minutes before, but this time, something began to hurt, the only thing that mattered to her, was being with David.

◆

VIV WRAPPED her cardigan around her shoulders. The copse somehow felt colder without the presence of David and Rosa. She sat anxiously on a small patch of grass in the hope Isabel would make her presence known.

*'Daddy's very proud of you.'*

Her little sister resumed her rightful place atop the little swing, almost touching the branches with the tip of her shoes by the time Viv turned to see her.

"Are you proud Isabel?"

*'Always.'*

Viv so wanted to walk over and touch her little hands, a simple gesture of affection. Yet she knew instinctively that a space was needed between them. It was an acknowledgement that her sister was indeed a Spirit. Yet the relationship at present was so natural and Viv wanted to keep it that way.

"Isabel, I'll be leaving soon. I wanted to say goodbye."

*'I knew already,'* she laughed and came to an abrupt halt. *'You can't go until you've been to the beach. Mummy and David are already there. I told Mummy it is very important. I want you to see something very, very special.'*

Isabel immediately leapt off the swing and came close, as if she were about to give a very stern warning and with a knowing expression began, *'You're very silly sometimes, especially for a big sister. There is no need to say goodbye because I am always with you. Not even the big beautiful sea can come between us,'* Isabel remarked proudly. *'Don't have a sad voice any more, you're late for a very special date,'* she sang merrily, *'Though you won't see me, I will be watching with you.'*

"I hope she gets here soon."

"Rosa, she will be here," David gently interjected. "Viv has been with Isabel, she would have told her to make her way to the beach."

Rosa wrapped her pink shawl tightly around her shoulders, the brisk salty breeze felt icy against her skin.

"I painted a picture of this very beach once and gave it to a friend back in England. I didn't realise it till now."

"You were meant to come here David. The painting was no coincidence. Maybe you were here in another life."

"Maybe," he said wistfully.

"Simon mentioned you many times David. You were special to him."

"He was a good man. He loved to chat for hours about Harleys."

Rosa brought a picture to her mind, then wiped the

tears from her eyes.

"Viv loves you very much David. I have to mention it because something tells me you are about to depart."

"She needs time to find out what she wants. I'll only cloud her judgement and influence her. I don't want to do that, even if it is unintentionally."

"I'm concerned David. She has a very special gift and if you leave she might not nurture it the way she should."

"She will," he replied, confidently.

"How do you know?"

"Because Isabel is with her."

Silhouetted against the rocks David watched as the topic of conversation slowly came into focus. Jogging gently across the sand, Viv dropped with a thud, beads of sweat rolling down her cheeks, "What have I missed?" she panted.

Rosa promptly wiped her face with a handkerchief.

"Nothing yet dear. David, would you mind if Viv and I have a moment – girlie chat?" she winked.

"I'm on tenterhooks," Viv replied, as David meandered over to the water's edge, "What do want to talk to me about?"

Rosa placed a canvas bag with pink embroidered flowers onto her lap, pulled out a white envelope and handed it to Viv.

"Open it."

Viv suspected it was a letter from her father. Perhaps one he might have written just before the accident. As she ripped open the envelope a wad of crisp 100-dollar bills fanned out before her.

"Rosa, what's this?" she asked, astonished.

"It is a present from your father and I. The one thing he regretted most was that his job never took him to as many places as he would have hoped. We had planned so many journeys together and he wanted to make sure that you got to see everywhere that he had planned to go. So we decided to set up a fund for you, as a gift. We did the same for Isabel."

"Rosa this is too much. I can't take this from you. Give the money to the church."

"This money is not meant for the church, it is meant for you. This is a whole new chapter in your life, your father and I want you to have the best possible start."

It was a truly wonderful gift Viv had not expected, she knew there was only one way to reciprocate the kindness.

"I want to tell you something that I've never told anyone before. I was involved in a car accident shortly before I left for America. I was in great danger. I stood transfixed in the middle of a country lane, powerless to get out of the way. I should have been hit. I would have died that night if I hadn't been pushed out of the way."

Rosa held Viv's hand very tightly.

"Isabel saved my life that night."

◆

IT CAN be said that God moves in ways beyond our knowledge and understanding. Sometimes we look for signs that don't appear and yet we know His guidance is ever present. Viv was sure that she believed in the presence of angels. The gentle tickling sensation in the palm of her hand was a sign her sister was with her. As Viv, David and Rosa huddled close on that sandy beach at sunset, the sky seemed to take on a life of its own. Though the sun was setting, a strange light filled their beach, like a million fairy lights were switched on, just for them.

"David, what's going on? The sky is so bright."

"I think my prayer has just been answered," he whispered. "I wanted you to see, as a final piece of proof, how powerful the Spirit world can be."

A magnificent white haze formed in the shape of angelic proportions. The billowy outstretched wings were silhouetted against the orange sky. Viv didn't blink for fear she would miss this wondrous spectacle.

"Viv, look how the angel is moving from side to side, just like a pendulum."

She acknowledged David with a quick nod of the head. Caught between a dream world and reality, it was impossible to define the time and place. Viv was with the angels now.

"You don't ever have to be afraid, Viv. You are looking at peace."

Viv squeezed David's hand tightly; it was all she could do to remain grounded. At that moment she could feel herself rise, floating above the ground, though common sense indicated she was stationary. She felt lighter than she had ever done before and a magnificent sensation of euphoria enveloped her entire being. She was being healed. The weight, which she had carried for so long, had been lifted off her shoulders. Viv was being acknowledged by the Spirit world.

"Are you happy, Viv?" she heard David whisper. She had her eyes closed gently, small speckles of light softly tickled her face.

"Finally," she replied.

She let the moment envelop her for a minute longer, then felt the light disappear. Her eyes opened and the beach was just as it had been. Rosa had her hands folded and seemed to be in prayer, Viv had to interrupt nevertheless, "Rosa he's gone. David's gone."

"He had to go Viv."

"Has he gone back to the hotel?"

The beach seemed so lonely now. The only person in sight was an old man strolling along the beach, minding his own business.

"He doesn't want me with him any more, does he Rosa?"

"Sweetheart, sit down and let me explain."

"I should head back and try to find him."

"He has gone Viv."

"What happened? I thought he was happy?" Viv pleaded, hoping Rosa would provide some semblance of an explanation.

"He is very happy, Viv. He's left because you've started on your journey now and need to take some time for yourself. He won't be gone forever. Look what he's left by your side."

A single yellow rose had been put in his place; Viv cradled the flower in her hand. Tears streamed down her cheeks.

"He was like an angel to me. Even now, he's still a mystery."

"He was."

"Will I ever see him again?"

"Do you want to see David again."

"Of course I do."

"Then you will. He is your earthly mentor; the two of you are strongly attached. Your father told me that you and David have actually known each other for aeons, in past lives. That kind of relationship cannot be lost or broken, you will certainly meet again."

As Rosa spoke her last words, Viv had a sense that everything had now been put into place. David was gone but she would see him again, she believed Rosa's wise words and took great comfort in the twilight of that early evening. From a small English village, she had travelled thousands of miles to understand her life, who she was, and what she could become. It was what her Dad had intended. Viv realised at that moment that he had been with her every step of the way.

Viv knelt on the wet sand and placed the yellow rose on a gently gathering wave. She set free all whom she loved but they were not gone forever. She had started on her spiritual path. For once, she allowed herself to feel happy at what she had accomplished and all she had yet to discover.

# About the Author:

THE EDITOR asked Stephanie to write something about herself. The following was quite unexpected but I think it just says something about where Stephanie is spiritually at this point in time and what she thinks about when she meets and encourages the people that she comes into contact with in her daily life:

### *Sorry I didn't make the time*

We all have busy lives. We all have stressful jobs and sometimes we can't make the time. Sometimes we just don't want to.

I wake up at 6am and have to be on the bus by 7.30am. My eyes are hardly open and yet I have to function as a human being. Remembering to be polite, to give the correct change to the driver and to give up my seat if someone needs it more than I do.

Talking is the last thing I want to do. I just want to crawl into my shell and pretend the world is still sleeping. I hide from familiar faces. I pretend that I am on an urgent call or in the middle of a gripping book, when really I am hoping they will disappear and not notice me.

One particular happy face likes to see me every day. I sneak to the back of the bus while the search for my face begins. Once he has turned away, I put my fake phone back in my bag and pray the bus is as swift as a magic carpet and delivers me to work without a blip to my early morning schedule.

I alight from the bus to be confronted by the happy face who questions why I had not said hello.

"Oh," I say, "I was reading my newspaper."

"How about a coffee? I have twenty minutes before I start work."

"Sorry," I say, "I have to start work early this morning."

He wishes me a good day and strolls off while I dart into the nearest newsagent and wait until there is a safe distance between us.

I amble to work with twenty minutes to spare. Minutes feel like hours. The early morning chill is a nasty wake up call. Coffee would have been a much nicer option.

The same routine of ducking and diving continues until one day, I have a new agenda, a new job and a new bus route. One last day with the happy face and one last chance to do the right thing. Only today, he is not on the bus. I realise that I miss the happy face and I cannot turn back time.

My early morning plan is thwarted, my conscience cannot be eased and I feel regret.

Lunchtime provides some relief. I eat my sandwich, guzzle my drink and hurry to the shops. It is there that I see the happy face. Working just like everyone else, facing the same stresses like everyone else and yet, never taking it out on anyone.

I move closer, feeling that now I can make amends, but my view is blocked and he is no longer there. I panic, glancing everywhere until I come face to face with the familiar.

"Hello, I haven't seen you in a while."

"Sorry," I say, "Sometimes I get distracted."

"I'm off on holiday next week so I won't see you on Monday."

"I'm starting a new job, so it's the last time I'll see you. Sorry, I didn't make the time for a coffee," I say.

"That's alright, it's just nice to see you."

And there it was. The happy face only wanted to say hello; to talk to me for five minutes before the monotony of the working day began. I had been so silly all those mornings. The fact was, I was glad to see his happy face.

Sometimes we take for granted what is right in front of us. Not returning a smile is an opportunity lost to make someone happy.

## Spiritual Philosophy Publishing:

Spiritual Philosophy has a mission. Our principal aim is to give first time writers of spiritual works the opportunity to get their books into print.

We want to encourage people of every age, gender, race and religious persuasion to enquire about Spirit. Every single person on this planet is important; every single person is different. It is for each person to develop himself or herself spiritually and it is for each person to find his or her own truth.

Many, many people are depressed, lonely and often question the reason for being on this planet. Through our books and monthly newsletter, we aim to help each person enjoy life and understand the wonder in balancing our material lives with our spiritual role. When the two are in balance, life is simply wonderful.

God bless you and welcome to our family of friends.

Visit us at:

**www.spiritualphilosophy.co.uk**

or write to:

SPIRITUAL PHILOSOPHY PUBLISHING
PO Box 79
Midhurst
West Sussex
GU29 9WW

Look out for our upcoming titles: